# TABLE OF CONTENTS

| | |
|---|---|
| CHAPTER ONE | 2 |
| CHAPTER TWO | 13 |
| CHAPTER THREE | 25 |
| CHAPTER FOUR | 33 |
| CHAPTER FIVE | 42 |
| CHAPTER SIX | 55 |
| CHAPTER SEVEN | 66 |
| CHAPTER EIGHT | 79 |
| CHAPTER NINE | 96 |
| CHAPTER TEN | 107 |
| CHAPTER ELEVEN | 115 |
| CHAPTER TWELVE | 132 |
| CHAPTER THIRTEEN | 146 |
| CHAPTER FOURTEEN | 78 |
| CHAPTER FIFTEEN | 86 |

# CHAPTER ONE

## A DISASTER IN DÖRFLI

Many years had passed since Heidi's American friends returned home.

On this clear spring day, Heidi, alone in her kitchen, was holding a letter she had just finished reading.

A cheerful April sun launched a mischievous ray through the glass and came to play on a resplendent copper pot.

Heidi was sitting at the table, her eyes captured in the vague distance, thinking. This letter, which brought her news of her friend Jamy, brought back old memories. What became of all those children who used to play, mischievous and happy, on the Alps, around the Alp-Uncle's cottage?

Margareth-Rose had just got married. Is it already possible! Georges had passed his engineering exams brilliantly last month and was immediately hired in one of the largest factories around New York. And what about Heidi's own children? Henry, after completing his studies at the Zurich Polytechnicum, has recently become deputy director of a major mechanical engineering company in Winterthur. Annette is currently taking the final exams at the Teacher Training College in Chur. Paul has stayed in Dörfli, attached to his land and mountains. He loves the rough and healthy life of the Alpine farmer.

He is a clever and lively helper for his father, Peter the gardener.

On this day Heidi felt very much alone in the old Manoir House, where Brigitte still faithfully serves her masters. She melancholically replayed in her mind certain events of her life. As a little girl -- she remembered the day when she and Aunt Dete climbed the path through the vineyards above Maienfeld. Then her thoughts lead her to Frankfurt: the whimsical silhouette of Mademoiselle Rougemont appears to her and makes her smile for a moment. What became of her friend Claire? Married, happy in the world; grandmother perhaps; who knows? It's been a long time since she knew where to reach her. Heidi remembered the old blind grandmother, the Alpe-Uncle and especially her great benefactor, Doctor Réroux.

Suddenly, she was pulled out of her reverie by a din of embittered little voices chatting animatedly in the village square. Heidi took a

look at the clock: three o'clock. Why were the children leaving school so early today?

Intrigued, she went to the doorstep and called out to little Lina, who seemed very agitated and concerned.

"Hey, Lina, come here and tell me what's going on."

Like a brood of little chicks to whom grain is thrown, the group of children rushes towards Heidi, chatting to one another. Everyone wanted to tell Heidi the big news and all of them shouted at the same time, so that it was hardly possible to clearly understand the reason for the trouble.

"Come on, calm down, children, if I know what you want to say. It's the teacher, I guess."

"He's sick," the whole gang of chatterboxes said in one voice.

"Sick? And what's wrong with him? Let Lina answer!"

"Madam, the teacher told us earlier that he wasn't feeling very well, that he couldn't go on with the class, and he dismissed us until tomorrow morning."

"How! Mr. Keller, sick?"

"He was coughing very loudly; it whistled as he took in breath," says a little boy.

"He was all pale, then he was all red," says another child.

"When we left, he sat in his seat, folded his arms on his desk, and dropped his head...."

"He looked like he was asleep; I saw him through the window ..."

Little Marie -- with the long blond braids -- said sadly "maybe he's crying because he's in pain?"

"Thank you for all your information," said Heidi, "I will go and see Mr. Keller and ask him if I can be of any help."

"Oh yes! Madam, thank you," said the children all together. And little Marie timidly ventured:

"Should we go back to class tomorrow morning?"

"Of course," replied Heidi. "And now, go home quickly, and above all be good."

The little group talked for a moment and then scattered.

Heidi took off her apron, put a shawl on her shoulders, a coloured handkerchief on her head, and went out. She met Peter, her husband, at the garden gate.

"Are you going out? Where are you going?" he asked her. "There hasn't been any misfortune, at least? You seem very concerned."

"I am going to the school to see how Mr Keller is. We had noticed in Dörfli that he had looked tired the last few days; he didn't look well. An hour ago he interrupted his lesson and sent the pupils home. Maybe he needs help."

"You are always the same, compassionate and ready to help. Ever since Mr. Keller lost his wife, he has been distraught. Go quickly."

"I will be back soon."

Heidi hastened her step, and her heart was beating fast. Poor teacher! He had to be at the end of his strength to abandon these little children he loved so much, to whom he had given the best of his heart for several years.

She knocked on the school door and, not hearing an answer, entered the classroom.

She found the old teacher just as Lina had described to her. She had a sad premonition.

Mr. Keller did not hear her come in. On tiptoe, she approached him and, gently, as one would do to a child in pain, she put her hand on his shoulder. The old man was startled, stood up, and, as if he had been at fault, lowered his eyes before the unexpected visitor.

"Mr. Keller, how are you feeling? It's me, Heidi."

He reached out his hand, which Heidi felt warm and clammy with fever.

"You shouldn't stay like this, dear friend. You should go to bed. You have a strong flu that makes you tired. Go back to your room quickly. I will send Brigitte to you. She will make a poultice and some herbal tea. That will make you feel better."

"How good you are, Heidi! You know I'm home alone. Since my only son François left us, in a moment of bewilderment, and since my dear wife died of grief, I have no taste for anything…"

"Come, come, Mr. Keller, we must act quickly."

"I don't have the strength anymore…"

A big tear ran down the hollow cheek of the teacher and got lost in his grey moustache.

"Do as I say. Get into bed. We don't want to, we can't leave you like this. Do you want me to help you upstairs?"

Mr. Keller started coughing very hard; a raspy cough that hurt Heidi.

Together they went up to the flat, above the classroom. At a glance, Heidi discovered the mess in the kitchen and the bedrooms. She didn't tell the teacher. It would have hurt him and could only have made his grief worse.

"There you go; lie down quickly. Brigitte will be here in a moment, and I'll come back in the evening to see how things are going."

She left quickly and returned to the Manoir House.

"Brigitte! Brigitte! Where are you?"

"Here I am," cried the old cook, out of breath. "What's wrong? I can't abandon my rissoles. They're going to burn! I've made a big fire in the cooker so that they'll be crunchy ..."

"Never mind your rissoles! Leave them there. I'll take care of them."

"But, will you tell me what's going on?"

"Mr. Keller is very ill. He has a cough; he has a fever and was unable to continue the class this afternoon."

"Poor Mr. Keller! All the misfortunes have been upon him for some time."

"Listen to me, Brigitte: take a muslin and a cloth from our kitchen cupboard. And also the box of dried flowers for the herbal tea. You should go to the grocery shop to buy flax flour and mustard powder. Then go to the schoolhouse and light a nice fire there. You'll prepare a hot herbal tea that you will make for a sick person to drink. Prepare a poultice and apply it to his chest. Come on! Don't be so stunned...."

"It is that.... Heidi... and dinner? Who will make our dinner?"

"Don't worry! I'll take care of it and I'll join you soon."

"Ah, well!" said Brigitte, as if relieved of a great weight.

"Come on! Move it! Listen again: while Mr. Keller holds his poultice on his chest, you will discreetly put the kitchen in order. A man alone, you see, can't tidy up the dishes like we can."

"Understood!"

Heidi went to the garden where she found Peter and his son Paul tending to some early geranium cuttings. She told them about what had just transpired.

"I have the impression," she said, "that our poor teacher is seriously ill. A nasty bronchitis like that can get very bad very quickly."

"Luckily the holidays are coming soon! He will be able to rest a little."

"But before the holidays there are exams. And Mr. Keller wants his students to respond brilliantly to the school board's experts. He will be worried."

"Bah! the examiners will be lenient; the circumstances are very mitigating."

"I'd have an idea," Heidi said, hesitantly. "But I'm afraid you won't approve, that you'll scold me."

"Your ideas are always good, dear woman; tell me what you are meditating on."

"I don't dare. I'm afraid I'll displease you."

"Say, anyway...."

"Well, this is .... If I was doing the class myself, instead of Mr. Keller, while waiting for a replacement? It will only be for a few days. It's for the children, and for him; and also for the good name of the school in Dörfli. You know how much I love the little ones; and after all, that's my job! I used to be a teacher. I am still missed in Hinterwald...."

She said it all in one go, as if she had feared not having the courage to finish.

Peter and Paul looked at her, taken aback. They both knew that Heidi had already made up her mind.

"What a curious idea," said Paul, after an embarrassing moment of silence. "You're not seriously thinking about it, are you, mother? I can see your great devotion and your tireless kindness. But you're not used to holding a class anymore."

"Of course, I knew that I would be scolded. I won't be any worse off than I was before. You know I haven't lost touch with my books. I still know enough to teach the little ones."

"We have no doubt about it," said Peter, "but that is not the main thing. In spite of your valour, you are not so young anymore; you will soon get tired. I know you: you will devote yourself entirely to your task. It is not only a matter of giving lessons, there's homework corrections and preparations for the next day besides."

"And who's going to keep us clean during those days?" Paul adds.

"And Brigitte? What do you do with her?"

The father and son didn't know how to answer. Moreover, they felt that any discussion was useless. Heidi left them.

"I'm going back to see Mr. Keller. While passing by the village, I will go to the post office; I will phone the doctor in Maienfeld, so he arrives tomorrow. I think that's better."

The two gardeners went back to work, pensive and worried.

The sun had just set behind the peaks overlooking Ragaz on the other side of the Rhine. The Falknis had taken on a golden hue and the Scesaplana glacier lit up for a moment in orange. Long purple clouds streaked across the sky to the west. A light fresh wind rose and the serenity began to fall.

"It will rain, tomorrow, maybe tonight. Enough work for today; put

away the tools, Paul. I'm going home."

Peter sat down in the kitchen, near the fireplace, calmly stuffed his pipe with the curved pipe, lit it with a brand and remained alone, immersed in deep meditation...

Suddenly Brigitte burst in.

"Peter! Peter! I think Heidi is losing her mind. She promised Mr. Keller that she would be in the class first thing in the morning until he gets better!"

"I know that," says Peter. "And it upsets me."

"She doesn't even want us to call a replacement. The Chairman of the School Board was there, proposing it. She talked so well and bamboozled him so that he finally gave up on the idea. I'm telling you she's losing her mind!"

And Brigitte went back to her stove, while Peter slowly drew puffs of smoke which he threw at the blackened ceiling. He barely heard Heidi enter, who was returning, radiant with joy at having accomplished a beautiful deed, but still a little anxious about the welcome her husband and son would give her.

"Well? asked Peter at last, breaking the silence."

"Are you mad at me? Say?"

"Oh, no! I don't blame you, although…"

"Although what? I can see that you are not happy. I've thought it over, be sure. I have my own idea…"

"Again! You see, Heidi, what I don't understand is why you didn't want us to call a substitute."

"Precisely because I have my own idea," Heidi repeated firmly. "You'll understand later."

## CHAPTER TWO

## A SAD DEPARTURE

The next morning the weather was gloomy. As the daily work resumed, the rain began to fall; a small cold rain that pierced to the bone.

Heidi went to the school house early. The old teacher had had a bad night. Brigitte, devoted, had stayed with him until midnight. He had a high fever and was coughing as if to crack his soul.

Heidi rekindled the fire, boiled some milk she had brought back and forced Mr. Keller to drink a cup of coffee and milk.

"This will do you good and give you some spirit, while you wait for the doctor to arrive."

"How good you are, Heidi, how good you are..."

He couldn't think of anything else to say. It could be felt that every effort hurt him.

A slight hubbub arose from the school hall, and the students' big sabots could be heard lightly hitting the flagstone floor of the hall.

"Ah! These children," says Mr. Keller in a choppy voice, coughing, "Aren't they adorable? Do you notice how gentle they are being?"

"They know you are sick and they may think you are sleeping."

"How nice they are! It's a change from ordinary days. What a rush at the entrance, before I appear! What a cheerful tumult that usually marks the beginning of the day!"

"It's time for me to go down and take care of them. There you go! I hear someone coming up the stairs."

There were a few timid knocks on the door and a crystalline little girl's voice shouted:

"Mr. Keller, are you asleep? May I come in?"

Without waiting for the answer, little Lina entered the flat, crossed the kitchen and stopped on the threshold of the bedroom. Her long brown cape, heavy with the rain she had received, was dripping on the floor. She remained there, planted, moved, surprised also to find Heidi at the bedside. What was going on in that little brain? The child was visibly impressed to see her master, usually so alert, motionless in a large bed. She didn't dare approach; she looked sadly at the face with its drawn features, the feverish eyes that almost frightened her. It could be felt that she was about to cry.

"Madam, I came to ask about our teacher; my classmates are asking if the lesson will take place."

"Yes, it will take place, this morning and afternoon, and all week long, until the Easter holidays," Heidi replied. "Come down and wait for me without making a racket."

"Come and shake my hand," said Mr. Keller.

Lina, feeling the value of such a call, understanding that she was on a mission, sent by her comrades, trotted to the bed.

"Give me your hand, Lina, and greet all the pupils on my behalf."

The schoolgirl suddenly opened her cape and put a small bunch of snowdrops in the burning hand of the patient.

"Here. I picked these for you on the way over. They are all wet and a little withered, because it is raining hard; I am going to fetch a glass from the kitchen; we will put them there. In the water, they will soon perk up."

The moment it was said, it was done.

"There," continued Lina "they will keep you company and maybe tell you stories, to make you better."

The hubbub was growing in the classroom. The pupils, finding the start of class delayed, began to get restless. Lina and Heidi went downstairs and entered the room together. The clothes hanging on the hooks smelled like a wet dog.

The child went to sit in her place and the new teacher, very comfortable but surprised herself to be there, struck the desk with her ruler. The lesson had begun... or rather was about to begin.

Heidi cast a glance around at all those stupefied little faces, penetrating sharply into each of the pairs of astonished eyes that looked at her strangely, not immediately understanding what was going on. She immediately grasped their feelings of natural astonishment, and in the pin-drop silence she said to them:

"My children, I can see in your eyes that you are surprised to see me here. I owe you a little explanation. I wholeheartedly wish Mr. Keller a speedy recovery, and you?"

"We do too," replied the children heartily, happy to break for a second the silence that weighed on them.

"I thought so. While waiting for this beautiful day, we could have brought in a replacement who doesn't know you, who would have asked for the way to a Dörfli he has never heard of. Perhaps - who knows - he wouldn't have liked you as much as Mr. Keller likes you. I know you all, and I like you…"

"So do we," said a choked little voice in the back of the classroom….

"That's nice, Louise. I'm sure we'll get along just fine. I must also tell you that many years ago I was a teacher in a small mountain village in the Valais; it is called Hinterwald. It is at the bottom of a valley, which valley? Who can tell me which river flows in the Valais?"

All hands were raised.

"Oh! Oh! You are all very clever. Tell us, Maria."

"It's the Rhône, Madam."

"Very good. So, Hinterwald is at the bottom of the Rhone valley, while our Dörfli is clinging to the slopes of a mountain overlooking another great Swiss river. Which one, François?"

"The Rhine, Madam."

"Very good. I see that Mr. Keller is teaching you geography admirably. In Valais, the landscape is almost the same as here, but a little more compact. The summits are just as high, the glaciers are bigger than the Scesaplana glacier. But in spring, as on these days, the flowers are as beautiful."

"Tell me, Lina; you brought a nice bouquet that delighted Mr. Keller's soul. Do you know what these little white flowers are called?"

Lina blushed to hear her friendly gesture revealed in front of all her comrades.

"Snowdrops, Madam."

"And yes, snowdrops; these delicate yet sturdy flowers, which are the first to bloom when the snow melts on the edges of meadows. Lina, do you know the story of the snowdrop?"

"No, ma'am."

"Which of you know it?"

No one raised their hand.

"It's a beautiful story. Since you are so wise, this morning, I am going to tell you this curious legend: Since it is the month of March; everywhere there is festivity in the air. April is secretly preparing for its arrival.

"However, under the snow, hundreds of flowers lying down are waiting impatiently for the moment to show themselves in full light. The trolls can't wait to blaze their shining gold; blue, purple or yellow gentians stand next to anemones, primroses and shy snowdrops. Despite their desire to get out of the wet earth, not a single flower dares to venture outside for fear of freezing to death. Finally, the snowdrop, the first, has the courage to stand up on its stem and look around. It is then dazzled by the sun, which gives it a friendly greeting...

"Look, little friend, nature is about to adorn itself in its beautiful finery. The hawthorn and cherry trees have their pretty buds ready. The snow will soon be gone. Go tell your friends the flowers that I am waiting for them so that the meadow will be smiling."

"The snowdrop still watches nature for many hours as it cleans itself in the spring; in the evening, it retreats underground to announce the good news to its timid and frightened companions."

At that moment, someone knocked on the classroom door.

Heidi opened. A young man dressed in black entered. The children all got up at once; they all knew the newcomer, the doctor, from Maienfeld.

"Hello, children; I have just visited your master. He is very ill. Madam, may I say a couple words in particular, without disturbing you?"

"Very easily, Doctor. I will dismiss the students for a moment. My little friends, it's time for recess. It has stopped raining. Go out into the courtyard, have fun but don't make a racket, so as not to bother Mr Keller, who is resting. Go on!"

The pupils went out, unhurriedly and with as little noise as thirty or so small farmers with sabots could make.

When the class was empty, the doctor said seriously.

"Madame Heidi, our patient is seriously ill."

"Truly? Poor Mr Keller! And what does he have?"

"I fear pneumonia. I have checked him thoroughly. There is no doubt about the diagnosis."

"What are we going to do? He is now all alone. It will be impossible to find someone to take care of him in the village. If only I were younger, or if Annette, my daughter, were here! She is taking her final exams at the teacher training college in Chur currently; we can't think of bringing her here."

"There is a solution."

"What is it?"

"To take our patient to the hospital in Ragaz, where he can receive all the care he needs."

"That would be the wisest thing to do, but how do we transport him?"

"It is easy to find a comfortable enough carriage in Dörfli. Here's what I propose: as I have to go and visit old father Hans again in a cottage on the road to Lutzensteig, I can be back here in a couple of hours, around eleven o'clock. You will have a carriage ready in front of the school and I will drive Mr Keller to the hospital myself.."

"What will he say when he knows he has to leave his Dörfli?"

"Don't worry, just now I prepared him gently for this eventuality. He is expecting his departure."

"Would you do me a favour, Doctor?"

"With pleasure, Madam."

"On your way out of here, stop by my house. Ask Peter to prepare our carriage for the hour we say, and ask Brigitte to come to school. My son, Paul, will drive you to Ragaz, and Brigitte will prepare the small items that Mr Keller would certainly want to take with him."

"All right. See you soon. Goodbye, Mrs Heidi."

Heidi accompanied the doctor to the gate of the courtyard; small groups of children had formed; the pupils whispered to each other; the teacher's illness, one could guess, was the subject of their lively conversations. Heidi went up to Mr Keller for a moment to inform him of the decision taken. She waited for Brigitte, who arrived after a few minutes; she gave him all the instructions, went back down to the pupils and clapped her hands. The children went back to class and took their seats.

***

When leaving the school, the pupils saw the carriage stopped in front of the gate. Paul and Peter were having serious discussions with the doctor; and they entered the house. A moment later Brigitte got out, carrying blankets and a pillow, which she artfully arranged in the carriage so as to make the patient's journey as comfortable as possible. Mr Keller, very pale, went out in turn, supported by Peter and Paul, followed by the doctor and Heidi, each carrying a suitcase. The small procession sadly crossed the courtyard. Keller got into the carriage with the doctor while Paul took his seat.

The children and a few Dörfli residents had formed a circle in the small square. Suddenly, softly, without anyone knowing how it had happened, a song rose up in the pale, melancholy light of that grey April day. It was the pupils, it was Dörfli who, in his own way, greeted the departure of the old teacher.

> At a time when the shadows are winning
>
> The slopes of the valley
>
> I see mountains
>
> The elusive horizon;

I hear the melody

From the evening bell,

I hear his blessed voice

Talking about hopeful love

Then when silence comes,

And that the day is dying

His singing with power

Calms my heart again.

Paul touched the horse with the end of his whip, the carriage shook and drove away, while the children, some with tears in their eyes, waved their hands in a left-handed gesture of farewell…

## CHAPTER THREE

## A USELESS LETTER

The end of the week went by, dull and rainy. Heidi, with her class finished, returned home each evening where the two men, who had stopped gardening in the bad weather, were bored in the house which seemed empty to them.

Peter, usually so cheerful, became moody, and moaned about the slightest matter.

"Paul, my son, I understand your mother less and less. We don't know how long this intolerable situation can last with her!"

"Next week is Holy Week, Dad. The school will be closed on Thursday, and Mum will come back to us for good."

"We haven't heard from Mr. Keller; that worries me."

"No news is good news, says the proverb!"

"I hope you're right! Did you know that the school board has asked the cantonal education directorate to postpone the exams until Mr. Keller returns?"

"I hope that the Council of State will accept, because mama might well get it into her head to carry out the test herself."

"I find her tiring. She's really unreasonable."

"She doesn't know, or doesn't want to rest. Lady! Standing up all day long to about thirty gallopers, going home and taking care of the housework; and then spending the evening correcting notebooks, preparing her lessons for the next day!"

"She won't be able to resist it for long. As you just said: it's a good thing the holidays are coming soon."

"I can hear her coming back."

"Hello Peter. Hello Paul!"

"Hello, Heidi!"

"Hello, mama!"

"Another day gone by. And very tiring! This damned rain that falls all the time forces me to keep the children in class during recess. It's like a zoo! My head will surely split!"

"You wanted it," said Peter in a gruff tone.

"More reproaches? By the way, still no news of Mr. Keller?"

"No."

"If we don't get anything tomorrow, I'll telephone the hospital."

Heidi entered the kitchen.

"Hello Brigitte!"

She doesn't have time to talk any more, Brigitte, very busy in front of her stove, suddenly turns around, as if a fly had bitten her.

"What a horror! It's already you, Heidi. What a misfortune!"

Heidi was taken aback, worried about such a welcome, and was nervous and questioned:

"What is it, Brigitte? I noticed that my husband and my son looked very funny; what misfortune are you talking about? What are you talking about? Is it Mr Keller, or is it Annette, who didn't pass her exams? Come on, talk!"

"No! No! Forgive me, there is no harm! No misfortune…"

"But then, explain yourself!"

"I was making waffles to surprise you. You came back earlier than usual, and there will be no surprise. That's why I said: what a shame!"

Heidi is breathing, but her emotion has made her feel tired; she pulls up a stool and sits down. Brigitte, meanwhile, puts some dough back into the iron which she heats on one side for a few minutes, then she turns it over quickly and skilfully, leaves it on the fire for a moment, opens it and takes out two golden waffles; she puts them on a plate and sprinkles them with fine sugar.

"Here, Heidi, you've earned them."

And while the lady of the house tastes the crispy pastry, Brigitte dares to say:

"Heidi, you look tired."

"You too?"

"How, me too? No more than usual."

"No, that's not what I mean; you too, like Peter, like Paul, are reproaching me. I may be a little tired at the end of the day; it's natural, I'm not twenty anymore, like in Hinterwald! But you can't imagine how happy I am to be in the midst of all these children. This contact makes me both younger and older at the same time. It seems to me that I'm doing my apprenticeship...."

"Your grandmother's apprenticeship," says Brigitte, bursting out laughing. And she continued:

"Dinner will be ready soon. I will set the table."

The evening meal was less melancholic than the previous days.

***

The next morning the daughter of the postal store manager came to class and gave Heidi a letter.

"Here you are, Madam. Father thought it should be brought to you right away. If he had brought it to your house, you would not have found it until noon on your way home. He recognised Mr. Keller's handwriting."

It was a poor letter written in pencil, in trembling handwriting, a sick letter, written

in a bed of suffering. Heidi read it quickly and said to the schoolchildren:

"Listen, my little ones; Anne-Lise has just brought me some news from Mr Keller. What he writes to me is sad. He is not much better. He still has a fever and coughs a lot. The doctor says it is pneumonia, and pneumonia is serious."

The children's faces were appalled. A heavy silence weighed on the class for a moment. Hans, a mischievous little man, raised his hand. "What a joke he's going to make again." Heidi wondered, hesitating for a second to give him the floor.

"Hans, what do you want?"

"Madam, couldn't we send a letter to Mr. Keller on behalf of his students?"

"We would all sign it," says Anne-Lise.

"That's a nice idea you have; which of you offers to write to Mr. Keller on behalf of all of us?"

All hands were raised.

"Me, me", said thirty voices at a time. "Me, me, Madam."

"I'm embarrassed! I'll make you a proposal. All of you are going to compose a project. Together we will choose the best one, we will have it copied by the one who has the best handwriting, and we will send it to Mr. Keller. You will all sign it, and so will I."

And in the following days, most of the lessons in the Dörfli school were spent reading the thirty draft letters. Even at recess, when they stopped playing games, the pupils discussed them among themselves; and again when they left the classroom, and also in the evenings at home. All the families in Dörfli took part in the preparation of the "Letter to Mr. Keller". New ideas, new words and ready-made sentences were created around the kitchen and dining room tables.

Time passed. On Tuesday, Heidi concludes this exciting writing exercise.

"My children, the letter must be finished tomorrow afternoon. Thursday is the beginning of the holidays, and we will no longer be together. None of the plans, as you yourselves have acknowledged, completely satisfy us. We will write these lines together, with the collaboration of everyone."

Poor Heidi! She needed prodigies of firmness, tact, diplomacy and persuasion to complete the task at hand. Everyone had a turn of phrase, a thought, often an original one. All of them, admirably, gave their hearts out. Finally, the final text was agreed upon. Heidi imagined dictating it to everyone, announcing that the most beautiful copy would be signed by the thirty pupils and sent to the old teacher. It had also been decided that, as it was soon Easter, a basket containing a bouquet of flowers, a few apples, a small cheese, dyed eggs and waffles made by Brigitte would be enclosed. "No nuts, they make you cough, and no cigars," said Heidi, who began to dictate.

"Dear Mr. Keller,

"It was with great sorrow that we saw you leave a week ago. Since then, every hour, every minute, we have been thinking intensely about you. We wish...."

Heidi was interrupted in her dictation by three loud knocks at the door. The postman brought a telegram. He whispered a few words in the teacher's ear, who suddenly turned pale, and left quickly.

The thirty little heads stood up and fixed their big clear eyes on the Mistress. Thirty glances, first intrigued, then worried, then anxious.

Heidi, visibly troubled, opened the yellow envelope and read the green paper. The children didn't even dare to whisper to each other, sensing a misfortune. Heidi pulled herself together, stiffened, and slowly, weighing her words, announced. :

"We must interrupt our dictation here.... We will not send the letter..."

She stopped. The syllables couldn't come out anymore, it seemed. She sat down. The pupils were eagerly awaiting the rest of the explanation; some didn't understand what bitterness the telegram could contain; others had guessed it, and stealthily wiped a tear from their eyelids. Heidi, now no longer mistress of herself, continued:

"We won't send the letter... It's useless now. The telegram brings us very sad news: Mr. Keller, your teacher, will not suffer any more. He died this morning in Ragaz hospital. I am very sad; he loved you so much."

She could not continue. Constrained by the tragic certainty, the girls began to cry, some of them with tears, some of them even with loud sobs. Little Hans also cried like a girl. The boys, prouder, but no less sensitive, tried not to betray their intimate emotions: some looked out of the window, others, leaning against their tables, supported their chins with their hand, did not take their eyes off the ceiling, others still, with their eyes lost in the haze, pretended to reread the first sentences of the letter that had become useless..... Heidi, for the first time in her life, did not have the strength to react. Her grief was deep. She was having trouble coming to her senses.

She dismissed the children and arranged a time for them to return in the afternoon, the last afternoon of school.

# CHAPTER FOUR

## SORROWS AND JOYS

At two o'clock, the class resumed in a very different atmosphere from that which would have reigned in normal times, the day before the holidays. Heidi announced that the exams would be postponed. The books, notebooks, ink fountains and other school materials were put away in the cupboards for a few moments. When everything was ready for the dismissal and the students had returned to their seats, Heidi said:

"Life, as you will gradually learn - some of you already know, alas, already - is made up of joys and sorrows. No one knows when the good Lord will call them back. Mr. Keller has left this earth; it is a great sorrow for us, but it is surely for him a great joy to be with the good Lord. You see, my children, do as our old teacher did, who never forgot our good Lord, so that he will not forget His servant either."

In saying these last words, Heidi had closed her eyes. The children thought she was praying. In truth, she had had a vision that quickly crossed her mind. She suddenly remembered saying the same words to Uncle de l'Alpe when she returned from Frankfurt as a little girl. In a few seconds she remembered Claire's grandmother, she relived the chalet, the fire, Doctor Réroux.... Brigitte was right the other day when she said that Heidi was doing her apprenticeship as a grandmother.

Heidi opened her eyes again and returned to reality.

"I will certainly not be the one to teach in Dörfli after the holidays. A new teacher will come; may he love and understand you like Mr. Keller!...." Heidi added in a whisper

Then, suddenly changing her tone, with an almost cheerful air, she added:

"Here are the holidays; beautiful holidays! Make the most of it. Be nice to your parents, help them, you boys, with the work on the Alpe, you girls, with the housework."

We don't want to leave each other like this, melancholically. I thought I would please you by devoting the few remaining moments to reading a story.

When you are older, you will probably go on an excursion to Freiburg, the picturesque city whose foundation I have told you about by the Duke of Zahringen.

Not far from Freiburg, at the foot of beautiful mountains, lies the most picturesque lake imaginable.

What a joy it must be to sail dreaming on its peaceful waters, it is an idyllic place. It is surrounded on all sides by rich pastures where large herds graze, and by lush meadows full of flowers.

One morning, a young child...."

The reading was suddenly interrupted by light knocks on the door.

"Come in!"

A beautiful young girl, smiling, appeared in the doorway.

"You, Annette!" cried Heidi, happily surprised. "You're back. And your exams?"

"Success, Mom, success! I received first place!"

"Give me a kiss, big girl. How did you find me so quickly?"

"The postman told me everything; why didn't you write to me that you had become a teacher again?"

"I didn't want to trouble your spirit in the midst of the commitments you have had to make lately."

"The postman also told me about Mr. Keller's sad end. You look tired, my poor mother."

"This is the last lesson I'm giving. I had just started reading a beautiful story when you came in."

This unexpected dialogue upset the schoolchildren, as it had prevented them from hearing the rest of the legend that had already captivated them. Heidi and Annette saw in the children's eyes the fear they had of not knowing the end of it.

"What story were you reading, Mum?"

"That of the swans of the Black Lake."

"It is very beautiful."

"Do you know it?"

"I know it by heart."

"Life is made up of sadness and joy, I said to these children earlier. I couldn't have said it so well. I was very saddened this morning when I learned of the death of the old teacher, and at this moment I am very happy. It's too much in one day. I feel very tired!"

"Poor Mummy! I have an idea."

"Which one?"

"Let me tell this story to the schoolchildren of Dörfli."

"Bravo! This will be your teaching debut."

And, turning to the children who were getting impatient :

"My little ones, it is Annette who is going to continue for you the story that has begun. You want her to, don't you?"

"Yes! Yes!"

Reassured and joyful, they clapped their hands.

Annette glanced at the book and Heidi pointed to where she had left off.

Annette, very at ease, in a fresh, happy voice, said:

"One morning, a young child was sitting by the fountain in his father's cottage. He detached wild carnations from their stems and threw them one by one into the pond. He was having fun watching them float by when a beautiful butterfly with cardinal red wings landed on one of the flowers. He set it in motion: the insect's wings resembled the sails of a tiny boat. Suddenly the carnation sank and the butterfly rose into the sky. The child went after it. The insect, which seemed to taunt him, let the child approach it, landed on a flower and then resumed its flight. He led the young boy to the shores of the Black Lake, passed over the calm surface of the water and disappeared into the dark forest.

Sorry and tired, he sat down in the shade of a fir tree and fell soundly asleep. In a dream he saw the red butterfly coming back towards him, fluttering by his side to cool the air he was breathing. Three angels presented him with luminous bouquets that seemed to be made of stones, while doves smoothed his long curly hair with their beaks.

He was suddenly awakened by a strange noise. Swans pulling a raft were moving towards him, through the reeds that bent down before them to let them pass.

O wonder! The child throws a few crumbs of bread at them. Since he could not capture the red butterfly, he would like to take one of the big white birds, but it is in vain that he tries to grab one by the neck. The swans retreat. He then embarks on a raft and the wind pushes him into the middle of the lake. The sight of the shoreline moving away made him cry out in fear.

At his weeping, the swans approach and surround the raft as if to keep the imprudent little sailor company. But he, despising all danger, leans forward to seize the most beautiful of the swans, when suddenly he loses his footing and disappears into the depths of the lake.

*He woke up in a velvet bed decorated with fine lace and realised that he was in the room of a mysterious fairy castle, just like the one his mother had often described to him. Three fairies watched over him. Their faces were as white as lilies and their eyes were black as night. They looked strangely alike and were also sweet and good looking. When they approached the child's bed, they said to him:*

"Have no fear, you foolish boy. Do you want to stay with us? We'll tell you stories, and to amuse you, we'll give you a log, parrots and a horse that will take you for a walk in our vast gardens. But you must think carefully before answering, because if you live with us for three days you will not be able to breathe the earth's air."

"Where's the pretty horse? exclaimed the delighted child, without worrying about anything else.

"He's waiting for you at the stable," the fairies answered.

"So I'm staying," concludes the child. "Let's go quickly to the stable."

They passed through several suites. There was nothing but riches and splendor everywhere. They arrived at a marble stable where twelve grooms in livery surrounded a young courier. A squire saddled the horse, and put the child on it. The animal trotted through shady alleys: the amused and happy fairies followed the horseman and steed on this charming walk that lasted more than an hour. On his return, the child asked them :

"Where is the good Lord?"

*The poor boy thought he was in Heaven.*

***

Several months passed in this way. The child made new discoveries every day. However, after a while, he became nostalgic for the family cottage and a deep sadness took hold of him. In vain the fairies asked him about the reasons for his grief. The child did not answer. He had promised his benefactors that he would never leave them, and he didn't want to hurt them.

One day, after an excursion of several hours under the green arches of the park, he lay down at the foot of a hill and cried bitterly, giving free rein to his darkest grief. Exhausted with fatigue, the poor boy fell asleep. The goddess of dreams touched him with her magic wand. In a dream he saw the cottage he had left, his father and mother still looking for him. He also heard the wind blowing through the fir-tops, the bleating of the merry herds of goats and the soft music of the bells of the Black Lake chapel ringing the Angelus. He woke up with a start when he called his mother. Suddenly he thought he heard her name. He got up and turned around; he saw a wrinkled old woman with hollow eyes and a pointed chin, walking with the help of a stick. This horrible woman approached him. The child shivered with fear and tried to run away. He was so frightened that he could not make the slightest movement.

"Handsome child," yelped the old woman, "since you're terribly bored here, I'll take you back to your parents. However, I have only one condition: that they keep me with them for the rest of my life."

"Never, never," cried the child, "I will never abandon my fairies!"

At these words, the witch disappeared in a luminous cloud. One of the three fairies who had heard everything approached him and said:

"Since you are faithful to your promise, tomorrow your wish will be granted, you will see the chalet where you were born again."

"Oh thank you! good fairy," replied the boy.

However, the pleasure of seeing his family again was diminished by the regret of leaving the three fairies, and he spent a restless night. When he woke up the next day, he was lying in the shade of the fir tree where he had fallen asleep a year before. The three swans were swimming in the reeds of the lake. He threw wild blackberries at them. The birds greeted him graciously and disappeared under the wave. The red-winged butterfly, which seemed to come out of the water, flew towards the mountain. The child chased it, and the insect, flying from flower to flower, brought him back to its parents' cottage and disappeared into thin air. The whole family greeted the young boy with the joy that we would expect and thanked providence for returning him to them.

When you pass by Lac Noir, you may see a child sitting on the shore trying to catch a glimpse of three fairies or three swans in the distance.

*However, neither fairies nor swans will show up. Only sometimes, on beautiful summer evenings, does he hear a soft whisper. This is the sad romance of the fairies singing under the waves.*

"Such is, my children, the legend of the swans of the Black Lake. And now all that remains for me to do is to wish you a happy holiday."

After shaking hands with Heidi and her daughter, the schoolchildren left the school light and cheerful.

Outside, the rain had stopped. A ray of sunshine was playing with the water on the fountain.

## CHAPTER FIVE

## NICE HOLIDAYS

In the mountains, the Easter holidays last three weeks.

On the Alps, the first appearance of spring has a very special charm. Thanks to the bountiful rays of the sun, which become warmer every day, the flowers gradually conquer the land. The snowdrifts and crocuses bravely force their way through and seem to push back the snow stains that stubbornly remain in the hollows. Irresistibly the white, mauve or yellow mass of flowers settles in the still brown meadows and then climbs to the highest pastures. Under the coppices, the anemones invade every damp corner. Nature is celebrating.

There was also joy at the Manoir House. Annette's parents were happy with her academic success, and Paul was proud of his older sister.

On Easter evening, the whole family gathered in the common room. On the wall, the old Uncle de l'Alpe, painted by Chel, was smiling in his frame.

We were chatting. Annette laughed happily at the idea that she would be called "Mademoiselle" from now on.

Heidi was shedding memories of her months of teaching in Hinterwald. She told once again about the difficulties of the beginning, how she had taught the girls to wash, comb their hair and then sew.

"Tell us about Chel, mother," says Annette.

"Training this little savage was my greatest joy! When I remember the visit to the cave that served as his lair, and when I look at the portrait of Uncle de l'Alpe that he later made from a photograph, that's when I can measure the full extent -- the value of the conquest of a heart, a soul, a spirit.

"It's a good thing there aren't many Chels in the school community," says Anne.

"My daughter, you will surely meet one of them, once or twice in your career. The secret, you see, to succeed in your new profession is to know how to put yourself in your students' shoes."

"Annette," Peter continued, "we are very satisfied with your work, and we are proud of your success. That deserves a reward. Tell us what would make you happy. We know you are reasonable; you will not ask for something that our means would not allow us to offer you. Think about it and make a wish; it is granted in advance."

Annette answered without hesitation :

"I don't need to think for long. My friend Jeanne, whom I have often told you about, and who graduated at the same time as me - she came second - spends her holidays at her aunt's house near Lugano.

When we parted on the platform at the station, she invited me to visit her, saying that her aunt would welcome me with joy."

"And what did you answer?" asked Heidi.

"That it was impossible, that the journey was expensive and that you were waiting for me to help you here."

"You are not very demanding, my dear child. It is granted: you will go to Lugano. When are you leaving?" he added mischievously.

"Right away, goodbye!" replied Annette, bursting out laughing. "Oh! Thank you! How kind you are. What a pleasure it will be for me to see Ticino. And in its best season."

"We owe it to you; it's not much, by the way."

"And while you're away," Heidi added mysteriously, "we're preparing a nice surprise for you."

"What is it, Mum, tell me!"

Shhh! Let's be serious. When are you planning to leave?"

"I will first write a quick note to Jeanne to inform her of your permission. The mail leaves in half an hour. She will have the letter tomorrow. I will have her reply on Tuesday or Wednesday. If her aunt accepts me, I'll be in Lugano on Thursday! We still have ten days left, ten long days, ten beautiful days to spend together!"

Annette, that evening, full of joy, and also awash with various feelings, found it difficult to fall asleep.

***

The next morning at 7 o'clock Heidi entered Annette's room. The girl was still sound asleep. Her mother woke her up with a kiss on the forehead.

"Annette Annette, a telegram! It comes from your friend Jeanne, who is waiting for you as soon as possible. I looked at the railway indicator. A train passes through Maienfeld at 10:12. You change at Thalwil, then at Arth-Goldau, where you have a 55 minute stop, time to eat properly, without hurrying. You take the Gotthard Express at 1.27 in the afternoon, and at 4.30 you are in Lugano."

"Oh, dear mummy, how happy I am," said Annette, jumping at Heidi's neck.

"Don't waste time. Prepare what you want to take away."

"As little as possible!"

"I'll serve your breakfast and then I'll help you pack your suitcase. Come to think of it, it would be appropriate for you to telegraph your friend Jeanne, to advise her of your arrival.."

"It is even essential. She has to pick me up at the station and take me to her aunt's house. I know that the village is called Dino! I don't know anything else!"

"Come on, get washed up. We'll chat over lunch."

***

Jeanne had come to wait for her friend on the platform of the Lugano train station. When she reached the esplanade overlooking the city, Annette was filled with wonder. The lake was deep blue. Monte Bre and San Salvator stood on both sides of the Ticino city with their dark green mass.

"How beautiful," cried Annette. I would never have imagined such a splendid landscape. What light! What colours! It's a real feast for the eyes that you have prepared for me, my dear Jeanne.

"It's very different from Chur... or Dörfli!" says Jeanne with a smile.

"We are going to have a wonderful time."

"A real holiday!"

The two girls went down to the lake. Jeanne did some shopping in the tiny boutiques nestled under the arcades of the old rue Centrale. Then they settled down on the terrace of a pastry shop while waiting for the departure of the tramway which, in one hour, would take them to Dino, on the slopes of Monte Bré, almost at the foot of the Dents de la Vieille, whose jagged rocks were looming on the horizon.

Annette wrote an illustrated postcard to her parents in lively colours.

From the tram trailer where they had taken their seats, the two young girls during their journey admired the palm trees, the magnolias in bloom, the chestnut trees making dark spots on the light of the spring greenery.

They arrived in the picturesque Ticino village at sunset. The spectacle was grandiose. The vastness of the sky became more and more intense. Annette filled her eyes with this unforgettable spectacle.

***

Ten days later, Annette returned to Dörfli on Sunday evening, very late. The village was already sleeping under the splendidly starry vault of heaven.

Heidi was the only one waiting for her daughter, "Mademoiselle Annette". She received her with undisguised joy and kissed her effusively.

"If you only knew how beautiful it was, mum! And how Jeanne and her aunt were nice to me. We went for a little boat ride on the lake, one day to Morcote, another time to Gandria, and even to Italy, to a little village called Campione."

"You can tell us all about it tomorrow. Tonight you are tired. Take this good cup of café au lait and these few buns; they will restore you. You must be sleepy."

"The journey is long, as you have to make a big diversion. I left Jeanne in Arth-Goldau. She was going to spend a few more days in Lucerne at her parents' house."

"I'm sure you're going to sleep well, girl. I won't wake you up in the morning. You're still on holiday."

"School starts again tomorrow morning in Dörfli. I'm thinking about it all of a sudden, has a new teacher been appointed?"

"Yes, a choice has been made, we received confirmation this morning from your father."

"Ah! Who is it? Where does this one come from? From the city? From the country? Was he at the Teacher Training College in Chur?"

"We will talk about all this tomorrow. Let's go to bed. Good night, Annette."

"Good night, Mummy. See you tomorrow!"

The next morning, Annette, for the first time in her life, woke up only around 10 o'clock. She was ashamed of her own laziness! She jumped out of bed. While she was washing herself, she felt a great emptiness inside her. She understood that one stage of her life was over, and that another was opening up, unpredictable. Against the wall hung her teacher's diploma in a brand new frame! Where would it lead her now? She would probably have to leave her Dörfli and her parents, whom she loved so much; like her mother, she would be called to some Hinterwald, perhaps for many years to come; God only knew. She was afraid of the future, of the unknown. She was ready to cry.

She went down to the kitchen, where Heidi and Brigitte welcomed her with radiant faces.

"There's my big girl!"

"Did you sleep well, Mademoiselle?" asked Brigitte with a knowing look on her face.

"Don't make fun of me, Brigitte!"

"What do you plan to do with your morning, rather than what's left of it?" asked Heidi.

"Is there anything I can do for you?"

"No, Mademoiselle!"

"You're annoying me with your "Mademoiselle!" or do you mean by that I'm no longer good for anything?"

"Nah!" says Heidi; "Brigitte teases you. Let's go to the village. I have some shopping to do. I'll go out with you."

Annette seemed upset. She would have preferred to go out alone. One thought obsessed her: Who was the new teacher in Dörfli? She didn't dare to ask her mother.

On the way, however, she took Heidi by the arm, to give herself courage, and asked :

"Wasn't school supposed to resume this morning? I see it closed, and the shutters of the teacher's flat are closed."

"Classes will not start again until this afternoon at three o'clock. There will be a small installation ceremony. The new teacher is said to arrive around noon only."

In the village square, a group of small children were play-making a tunnel in a large pile of sand. When they saw Heidi and Annette, they ran up to them and all at once held out their dirty little hands to greet them.

"Hello, Mademoiselle!"

"You mustn't say "Mademoiselle" to me, come on! Have you forgotten that my name is Annette?"

"No, M'zelle Annette," said little Lina, with a mischievous smile.

When they had freed themselves from the rowdy troop who had returned to their game and Heidi and her daughter were alone, Annette, impatient, said:

"Mummy, I don't recognise Dörfli any more! What do they all have to say to me, "Mademoiselle"? I would understand that from strangers, but here!"

"It's only natural, my daughter. The whole village knows that you have your teacher's diploma; everyone, big and small, is proud of you. This is their way of congratulating you."

At the grocery shop, Annette tried to find out more about the new teacher. She questioned old Adèle and little Thomy, and others who filled the shop.

"We don't know. We don't know him, we've never seen him."

That's all she could get. There was little to satisfy her curiosity.

At lunch Annette told about her holiday in Ticino and enthusiastically described the excursions she had made, the beautiful flowers she had seen in the parks of Lugano and in the villas by the lake. Her father took a keen interest in all the details, as they related to his profession.

"I grew some of these flowers when I did my gardener's apprenticeship in Maienfeld. Here, because of the altitude and the cool winds, they could only be grown in a greenhouse. These magnolias, tulips and curious passion flowers that you saw in Gandria would not find admirers in our poor Dörfli."

Paul then brought the conversation to the afternoon ceremony. Annette became emboldened.

"Tell me papa, you who are part of the municipality, you must know who Mr. Keller's replacement is."

"I just know his name. I don't know him, I've never seen him."

"I'm sure," says Annette, "that it will be a horrible man, severe and wicked, who will make the children unhappy."

Everyone smiled at this joke.

"I'm afraid you're right, my poor little one! It seems that he has decided to be harsh in this village."

Annette became red with indignation.

"We won't allow him to do that, and if he is too mean, we will send him home. First of all, why hasn't that naughty man arrived yet?"

"It won't be long now. It is already half past twelve."

"Is he married?"

"We don't know! You can ask him yourself," said Paul laughing.

"You're teasing; I'm sure it was all of you who chose it."

"He is said to be handsome," Paul says mischievously.

The meal was spent imagining the appearance of the one they were waiting on. Annette looked out of the window all the time. It seemed to her as if she had heard a sound of bells or footsteps on the road. Perhaps it was the new schoolmaster? Each time she was disappointed to see only a man from the village, or a farmer's cart.

"I think," she says, "that you have chosen a man who is too serious, who will never laugh and who will sadden the whole village with his cold and distant air. Oh," she added jokingly, "if you had asked me for advice, I would have been able to tell you what kind of teacher Dörfli is suitable for!"

"And what would you have chosen?"

"A cheerful, educated young man who loves children and the mountains. A city-dweller will not like us, and we will be unhappy."

"You talk as if you have to go back to school," Peter told him. "Let's hope that everything will work out, and that we won't be disappointed. You know that I am a member of the municipality. It's time for me to go and do a bit of preparation for the introduction of such an important person. In fact, you can accompany me and I will even ask you to take your violin to make the children sing."

Annette helped Heidi and Brigitte to clear the table and wash the dishes.

She pressed the two women so that everything in the house was in order. If it took the fancy of the newcomer to come and greet his kinfolk before going to school, the Manoir House had to make a good impression. A tuft of primroses picked in the neighbouring meadow would replace gentians which were no longer very fresh; Annette changed the tablecloth and redid the curtains. Then she went to her room. She put on a blue dress strewn with little red bouquets. She tied a white scarf around her neck; with a comb she only wore on special occasions, she fixed her two beautiful brown braids on her head.

# CHAPTER SIX

## THE SUCCESSOR TO MR. KELLER

Shortly before three o'clock, the whole family went to school. The new teacher had decided not to stop by the Manoir House, and Annette was disappointed. They did not meet anyone on their way. All the inhabitants of Dörfli were probably already settled in the large hall where the ceremony was to take place. As Annette entered the door of the house, she felt herself embraced by a strange emotion; she stopped frozen in place. The children were in their place, silent. At the back of the classroom, many parents, sitting or standing, seemed to be waiting. Near the empty desk, the members of the municipality in ceremonial clothes were speaking in a low voice.

All heads turned towards the new arrivals, the children stood up and, as if at a signal, a girl came forward, holding a bouquet, saying:

"Welcome to our new teacher!"

Unbelieving her ears, Annette looked back at her father and mother who were following her.

They smiled and nodded their heads.

Then, joyful and confused at the same time, Annette put the violin in the arms of the vicar and bent down to kiss the little pupil, who blushed with pleasure.

Solemnly, the President of the municipality, after clearing his throat, began the reading of his speech:

"Mademoiselle, I have the privilege and great pleasure to announce that, on the notice of our municipality and the School Board, the Council of State of the Canton of Graubünden has appointed you to succeed the late Mr Keller as a teacher in Dörfli and has entrusted you with the management of our school for one year on a trial basis."

He stopped, as if he was astonished to have been able to pronounce such a long sentence without a hitch. Then, resuming:

"On behalf of the City Council and on behalf of all the residents of Dörfli, I congratulate you on this well-deserved success. We are convinced that there could not have been a better choice..."

He stopped again, put the paper in his pocket, stroked his big grey beard, hesitated for a moment.

"My dear friends from Dörfli, dear children, and you, my great Annette. I had written a long speech, but now I feel how official words are not appropriate between us. It would have been appropriate if someone had sent us one of those young city-dwellers who don't understand anything about mountain people! We're lucky: you're one of us. You know better than anyone else what the school in Dörfli should be like. You graduated first in your class from the teacher training college, we are sure you are a scholar. As for advice on how to run a class, I'm not the one who can give it to you! It is Heidi, your good mother, who will guide you through the beginning of your career. You are lucky, and we are lucky too. Come and give me a kiss!"

Annette was very moved. So it was true, she was a teacher, and in Dörfli! Her dearest dream had come true! While parents and children applauded, the pastor and members of the municipality came to shake her hand and congratulate her affectionately.

Annette immediately took her role seriously and walked to the lectern and simply said:

"I am too happy and too grateful to give you a long speech. If you don't mind, I will thank you by having the children sing some of our beautiful mountain songs."

She tuned her violin, which the vicar had kept, and soon young and old alike were singing in their hearts about the beauties of their beloved homeland.

Then the adults went back to their work and the students were given time off to prepare the next day's work.

Remaining alone in the classroom, she sat at the desk and looked around. Everything had been changed in a few days: the students' tables had been freshly planed and the walls re-washed. The pulpit was brand new and very beautifully carved. Certainly her parents had been there. They had wanted their daughter to be comfortable in her clean and neat furniture.

So she felt her heart overflowing with gratitude and love for them. At the same time, the mystery of their conduct during the previous days became clear.

In the evening, she was teased a little.

Peter asked him:

"Was our choice so bad, my daughter? Is our teacher too serious?"

"I hope your choice is good, but I am a little afraid now that I am not serious enough, nor learned enough, for my task."

"God will help you if you ask Him," Heidi added. "I think you haven't forgotten to thank Him, first."

***

The next morning, at a quarter to seven o'clock, the school bell began to ring in a strange way. First there were three weak, hesitant blows, then a whole series of quick, irregular blows flew off the bell tower like bees in a hurry to get out of the hive. At home, the villagers raised their ears; some smiled, others frowned, but it became clear that the new teacher was struggling with the first difficulty of her profession: to pull the rope of the bell with regularity, without interfering with the beating.

Annette counted aloud: "27, 28, 29". She knew she had to ring thirty times, she knew it. So she counted "thirty" and let go of the rope. This produced a cascade of metallic sounds from above, in the bell tower, which filled the young teacher with anxiety. She grabbed the rope tightly to stop the noise, but she pulled too hard and the bell started beating again "31, 32, 33, 34…".

Annette, a little confused, entered the empty classroom, sat down in her place and immersed herself in the notes she had brought. She reread them distractedly while the pupils entered and settled down. Finally, she raised her head and looked around. At first she could not make out the faces clearly.

"I will call the roll. Upon hearing your name, each of you will stand up and answer 'Present'. Hans Annen."

"Present!"

Annette looked carefully at the stocky, stocky little guy; she knew he was the son of the forester.

"Alfred Bertschi"

"Present!" replied a tall boy, with a cheeky look on his face.

"Jean-Pierre Vernez"

"Present!"

When the boys' call was over, it was the girls' turn:

"Lina Weber"

"Present!"

"Anne-Lise Salits"

"Present!"

"Flora Castelli"

"Present!"

"Marthe Castelli"

"Present!"

The two voices that answered her were absolutely identical, and Annette, looking up, remained for a moment as if petrified with astonishment. She had two absolutely similar faces in front of her. The same dark blue eyes with black eyelashes, the same big laughing mouth, the same curly light chestnut hair. The young teacher suddenly remembered that in the last letter she had written to her, Heidi had mentioned the return to the village of the Castelli household and their two twins. The father, a bricklayer, had worked for several years in the towns on the Swiss plateau. He had returned to Dörfli with his family after the death of his in-laws.

Busy with her exams, Annette had read the news, but hadn't been interested in it.

She asked:

"Which one is Flora, and which one is Martha?"

The twins looked at each other, smiled gently and answered in one voice:

"Me."

All the pupils burst out laughing, and it made a deafening noise in the classroom. Annette was frightened; it seemed to her as if she was suddenly faced with a band of malicious little devils watching her every failure. Why hadn't the teacher training college in Chur prepared its students for such contact with twin pupils? Her question was a clumsy one; what could be said to restore calm?

"Flora, come here."

The noise stopped instantly and the schoolchildren became attentive. Their eyes sparkled, we were going to have fun. Flora stood by the pulpit and Annette stared at her to engrave the girl's features in her memory.

"Marthe, come here too."

The little one stepped forward and stood next to her sister. Annette looked at her, it was the exact portrait of her twin sister.

There must be a way to distinguish one from the other, Annette thought; you just have to look for it. Let's see... Flora's eyes may be a little brighter than Martha's; Martha may have darker hair than Flora...

But no! There was no sign to say for sure: it's Martha, it's Flora.

However, the young teacher, fearing that she would lose her authority by acknowledging her inability to distinguish between the twins, sent them back to their place by saying:

"That's good, now I know both of you perfectly well."

The two girls turned their backs to the lectern and went to their seats, one through the centre corridor, the other through the right corridor. They sat down with the same gesture, and Annette, looking at them, felt very troubled; where was Martha, where was Flora?

The reading lesson began. Annette had Alfred read, then Jean-Pierre; then it was Lina's turn. In this group of pupils aged twelve to thirteen, there were only the twins.

"The next one, now.."

Playfully, the two girls began to read together and the whole class burst out with a loud, sonorous laugh that could be heard all the way to the bottom of the village.

What were the villagers who passed by the square going to think? They would think that she had no authority, that the children made fun of her. Their opinion of the new teacher would be very bad, no doubt. "What to do, what to do?" the girl wondered anxiously. The laughter was accompanied by the sound of feet and banging on tables.

Suddenly, Annette was inspired.

"Know how to put yourself in the shoes of your students," Heidi told her. In a second Annette saw herself on a school bench and started to laugh too, looking at her class with a cheerful and well-heard look on her face. It was miraculous. After a few seconds, calm was restored, but the joy was still on everyone's face.

"I shall never distinguish Martha from Flora, nor Flora from Martha!" she said. "So to avoid scolding each other when the other has done something foolish, I am going to give you a sign every morning when you arrive."

"Yes, yes," shouted the children, "give them a sign."

"Which one? Ask Annette."

"A coloured ribbon."

"An eagle feather in the hair."

"A black spot on Marthe's nose."

Responses came from everywhere

"That's enough," says Annette laughing. I will choose a blue ribbon for Flora, and a red one for Martha. Every morning I'll put them in their hair, so I won't confuse the two sisters any more!"

And the lesson continued after this incident.

The task of the young teacher was certainly not always easy. There were thirty pupils aged between seven and thirteen, girls and boys.

Every evening, Annette went home and told Heidi the details of the day. The advice and encouragement from her mother was a great help to her.

"Know, my daughter, that the secret to success in your vocation is knowing the faults and qualities of each of the children entrusted to you."

"It's not easy with little mountain children; they don't give their hearts out at school."

"There is no doubt about it. It is therefore by means of individual interviews that you will be able to penetrate the soul and spirit of your pupils."

"I know this theory, my dear mother; how can I put it into practice?"

"You see, in Hinterwald, in spite of the hostility I had encountered, I had got to know all the families; I was interested in their work, I took part in their worries, in their joys. In a village it is much more convenient than in a big city. What's more, you are lucky enough to be from Dörfli, where the doors of every house are open to you. Go and see your pupils in their homes; and above all, love them all equally."

Annette followed these instructions. She soon became the oldest friend of the children of Dörfli, the wise counsellor of all of them.

With her gentleness and firmness she imposed her authority, gained respect and conquered hearts for many years.

# PART TWO

## CHAPTER SEVEN

### THE HAPPY FAMILY

Fifteen times already the high mountains, the valleys and the village have been covered by a thick layer of snow; fifteen times the pastures have turned green, the alpine flowers have brightened the meadows and the brilliant summer sun has once again covered the whole of nature.

Heidi is certainly no longer the alert young mother she once was, but the same charm still emanates from her person. She is still very often a troublemaker for others and knows how to share the sorrows and joys of others.

At the "Manoir", young Lina, who became an orphan early on and was taken in by Peter and Heidi, replaced Brigitte. She has just turned twenty-two years old. Lively, always cheerful, she assumes the direction of the house, surrounding her adoptive parents with affectionate gratitude.

Heidi is the grandmother of several grandchildren.

Henry is in New York where, thanks to friends from America who were regularly in contact, he has found himself in a nice situation; he married a Swiss girl born in Switzerland; he has a 12 year old son, Jean, and a 9 year old daughter, Elizabeth.

Annette married the doctor from Maienfeld; they have two children, eight-year-old twins, Jean-Pierre and Jacqueline.

As for Paul, who remained in Dorfli, he founded a home with Ida, the postman's daughter; a little girl, who is now five years old, and two boys, one four years old and the other who is still just a baby, run the "Manoir". Paul has taken over the horticultural work from his father. He has even created a splendid alpine garden where he has gathered all the flora of the region.

That morning - it is in the middle of May - Peter is sitting in the big armchair; he is reading an unfolded newspaper, behind which vanishes his face and the beautiful grey beard that frames it.

Heidi sits opposite him and knits a pink woolen brassiere for the baby. From time to time she takes some boiling water from the singing kettle and pours it over a fragrant coffee.

The two old men are waiting for lunch; Ida and Lina are busy in the kitchen, and the smell of food is appetizing.

Suddenly the door opens with a bang and two children burst into the room like two imps. Jean-Pierre tumbles on the floor, and slipping under the newspaper, jumps astride on his grandfather's lap. Jacqueline sits on the arm of grandma Hedi's armchair, takes her by the neck and embraces her with all her strength.

"What a pleasant surprise", says Heidi. "But you didn't go up to Dorfli on your own. Where's your mother?"

"She's behind us. She can't run as fast as we did. We left her at the edge of the village. She'll find her way by herself," says Jean Pierre with a mischievous look on her face.

"It's not nice to leave your mum on the road like that," said the grandmother.

"We did well on our own! Mum will do well too!" replied Jean-Pierre.

Peter and Heidi looked at each other, surprised at the response which touched on irrelevance. Jacqueline pressed her little head against her grandmother's cheek.

"Say, Grandma, when are we going up to the chalet?"

"Because, you know, we came to Dorfli to go up to the chalet; it's decided."

"It's decided, it's decided! How you go, my little man!" said Peter, surprised by such assurance.

Annette entered at this point, out of breath and showing some concern. She thought: God knows what pranks my two terrible ones will have done before my arrival!

"Hello Annette, what a joy to see all three of you here. It's sunny in the house!" says Heidi.

"Sunshine! Sunshine! I would rather talk of storms," smiled Peter, who had been trying in vain for some time to get rid of his grandson.

"Grandma, aren't we going to the chalet? Grandpa promised it on our last visit," shouted jean-Pierre, clinging to his grandfather's shoulders.

"I promise! It's all about getting along. First get off my lap and we'll talk more comfortably."

"I won't come down until you tell me when we'll climb the Alpe," Jean-Pierre answered, suddenly cajoling.

"As soon as your grandmother has packed her bags," and let go of Pierre recklessly.

The child slipped to the ground, as fast as lightning, and rushed towards Heidi.

"Oh! So, Grandma, we'll pack our trunks today! Please, let's do them right away, I'll help you and we can leave in the morning."

"Patience, for the moment, let's sit down at the table. Come with me to the kitchen to say hello to Aunt Ida and Lina; Paul will soon be back from the garden with Marie who is very interested in her father's work."

The meal went happily, amidst the laughter and chatter of the five children. Heidi, Peter, Annette, Paul and Ida were discussing among themselves how to accommodate all these people at the Alpen house.

"It's no secret to you," says Peter, "that last autumn I transformed our summer house. Your Alp uncle seemed to have planned, together with Doctor Réroux, the enlargement of this house."

"You haven't seen this masterpiece yet, Annette," Heidi added. "You won't believe your eyes. The chalet has doubled in length. We have extended the kitchen; the dining room is the old goat shed. I myself haven't been back up there since the work was completed."

"It's a real boarding house!" says Annette, laughing.

"You're right, a vast home for *our* family! We thought that if we squeeze in a little, soon we will all be able to live there."

"You are not unaware, my dear Annette, that the last letter we received from New York tells us of your brother Henry's intention to come and spend the summer in Switzerland."

"It is true that I do not yet know my sister-in-law from America, nor my nephew or niece from the New World!"

"Neither do we!"

"Yet we have seen them in photographs, says Jean-Pierre's little flute-like voice. Aunt Edith has a hat this high! And cousin Elizabeth has bare legs, with socks like the boys."

The meal was over. The children were sent to play in the orchard. Lina cleared the table and brought coffee. Ida went up to her room to put the baby to bed and he fell asleep immediately in his cradle.

"He's not shy, your Jean-Pierre," Paul tells his sister.

"My son is a son like the goats and curious like them."

"I pity his teacher in Maienfeld!"

"Let's pity his parents instead! Here's what might surprise you: at school, he's as tranquil as a painting. Since he has a lot of life to spend, once he gets home, he gives his exuberance free rein."

"He will be able to have a good time on the Alps," says Peter, who had lit a long black cigar.

"For some time now, Jean-Pierre has been passionate about going up to the chalet," says Annette. "He keeps asking me questions: 'When will we go up to the chalet? What is the chalet like now? Will I sleep in the same room as Robert and Jean when they come from New York?' It's a splitting headache."

"And your husband, what does he say about all this?" asked Ida who had come down.

"Claude is very happy about it. Remember what a pleasure it was for him last summer to spend a few days on the Alpe."

"Moreover", Heidi added, "he was the one who came up with the idea for this year's family holiday. It is thanks to his financial support that we were able to make the necessary changes. He will be surprised and satisfied, I hope, with the use we have been able to make of the Alpine residence."

"I think he will come up to us every Sunday, maybe even Saturday night already."

"What beautiful days we will spend up there, in the middle of nature," says Lina, pouring a second cup of boiling coffee for everyone.

"Heidi, a grandmother, surrounded by her seven grandchildren!" murmured Pierre with a touch of emotion. "What a splendid family picture!"

A silence of well-being and happiness reigned for a few minutes in the room. Everyone recalled this admirable vision of the near future. Paul stood up first.

"I'm going back to work."

"By the way, take a look at the children! You can hear them laughing in the bright sunshine."

Peter, after hesitating for a moment, ventured :

"Would I embarrass you by making you hear some beautiful music? This magnificent radio set that Claude gave us at the end of last summer allowed us to spend pleasant evenings this winter."

"Paul and Lina go to bed early," Heidi added. "Two old people like us don't need so much sleep any more and this instrument with its pure sound has given us beautiful concerts from Zurich to Basel, Geneva or even Paris. At times we have even been able to pick up the airwaves from New York."

"These Americans make very strange music, which we don't like very much! However, we listened to it all the same because it came from New York, and we had the illusion of being very close to Henry."

"In fact, it is the only post in the village, says Heidi. Last autumn, when the wind of madness was blowing across Europe, we were happy to hear the recent news! May the nightmare of the war that threatened have gone away forever!"

Peirre had turned the knob of the device. A sonorous and rhythmic Swiss air came out of it. The adults listened in silence.

Pierre gently beat the tempo with his foot. Heidi swung her head imperceptibly.

Suddenly Annette burst out laughing as she pointed to the window opening.

"I told you he was as curious as a goat, my Jean-Pierre!"

A small curly head emerged just at the height of the sill: on either side of this lively face, two little hands were clutching the stone. The man had left the children to listen to the music in secret. Seeing himself uncovered, he quickly walked around the house and entered the dining room, shouting:

"Say, Grandma, are we packing the trunks soon?"

"Ours is already done!" says Annette. "But it is still in Maienfeld. It will only arrive in the evening, by postal car."

"I don't think there's any point in you unpacking it," Heidi remarked. "You can just take what you need for the night. We'll go up to the chalet in the morning."

Jean-Pierre took a great leap, followed by a tumble so vigorous that the earthenware plates vibrated in the china cabinet and the cups clattered in the sideboard.

"Hurrah!"

And he went to the orchard to tell the children the great news:

"Tomorrow, tomorrow! It's on! It was Granny Heidi that said it! Tomorrow, we're going up to the chalet, on the Alpe!"

And grabbing the two closest children by the hands, forcing the fourth to close the circle, he led them in a frenzied round, shouting with joy.

The din was so loud that it woke up the little baby who, in his cradle, could scream at the top of his lungs, chorusing with his brothers and sisters and his cousin.

What a cheerful tumult! The old Manoir had never heard so much.

Breathless from having turned so fast, from having shouted so much, the troop rushed into the house, Jean-Pierre in the lead.

Heidi found it difficult to resist the onslaught of her grandchildren. They hung on to her skirt, pulling her from here, pulling her from there.

"Come, Granny, come with us. You'll take out everything we need to take away for the summer. We'll put it in the trunks. You'll see how quick it will be!"

Really, it was a great day! In an instant the Manoir House took on the appearance of a fairground stall. Clothes of all kinds were spread out on the beds, sofas and armchairs. Jean-Pierre and Jacqueline gathered in the middle of the hall, between the legs of a rocking horse, picture books, dolls, a spinning top, three snowshoes, two multicoloured feathered ruffles and a box of watercolours. Jean-Pierre unearthed another puppet, a little sheet bear filled with bran, a whip, and a whistle which he threw triumphantly onto the pile of toys, to the great dismay of his cousin Marie who feared for the existence of her dolls.

"That's it, that's it!" said Robert, Marie's little brother.

Indeed, "that was it"! In the Manoir, you couldn't sit anywhere anymore, and to get from one room to another you had to step over heaps of objects of all kinds.

"You're crazy, kids!" cried Lina as she came out of the kitchen. "It's true that one move is worth two fires."

"Well," says Heidi. "I'll take over as sergeant major…"

With prodigious skill, Pierre had managed to place three empty trunks, with the lid up, in the dining room.

It was then that Granny Heidi began her task, with admirable patience and gentleness Annette and Ida offered to help her. She refused their help.

"No, no. I have my plan! Just stay here and you'll have a great show…. Comical I suppose."

And she called:

"Jean-Pierre, Jacqueline, Marie, Robert! come to me."

The four came running and stood in a row in front of their grandmother.

"Isn't your greatest desire to go up the Alpe tomorrow?"

"Yes, Granny."

"Of course."

"We're counting on it."

"Naturally!" replied the children, together.

"Well, listen to me: on my own, I'll never be able to get the trunks packed tonight. You'll help me, like the grown-ups you are, and in less than an hour we'll be done!"

"Bravo, I'm going to get the dolls," shouted Jacqueline, rushing into the hallway.

"And I'll get the horse," said Jean-Pierre.

"And I'll get the whip," said Marie.

"And I'll get the whistle," sang the little Robert, who ran away.

Heidi, Annette and Ida started out laughing.

"It's off to a good start", says Annette. "How are you going to manage, my poor mother?"

"Never mind! You, Annette, you will go to my room and give the little messengers the clothes they will tell you from me. Ida will go to hers and do the same."

The children had returned, their arms full of toys that they had thrown into the first trunk that came along. Then they left to look for the rest.

"That way," says Heidi mischievously, "the vestibule is cleared and it will be easier to get through."

The grandmother, with art and method, ordered the transport of the clothes from the rooms to the trunks. The four children, conscious of the importance of their mission, carried out their task with care and eagerness.

By snack time, the trunks were made. The postman brought the fourth one, the Mayenfeld one, just as the children, sitting on the third one, put their full weight on the lid to pack the swollen clothes that prevented it from closing.

"There you go! That's it! You are real little mountain dwarves…."

"And you are the good fairy," Jacqueline said in a low voice."

"The good fairy will serve you a snack. You've earned it. Let's eat!"

# CHAPTER EIGHT

## THE WAY UP TO THE CHALET

The next morning, the first rays of sunshine had been casting their golden powder on the surrounding peaks for half an hour; already the four little devils were chatting in their room with volubility. In the trees of the orchard, in the damp freshness of the dawn, the sparrows were chirping, as if to give the reply. A tart horn blast resounded on the road, followed by the cracking of a whip alternating with a loud and joyful "yu-chee". It was Thomas the goatherd, who for the first time of the year was leading his herd to pasture. Jean-Pierre, Jacqueline, Marie and Robert rushed to the window to see the pretty spectacle. About twenty goats were ringing their bright bells, jostling each other, excited at the idea that they were climbing towards the freedom of the big rocks.

The weather was splendid. The day looked like it was going to be beautiful. The children greeted Thomas from the window with cries of joy. The little goatherd answered them, waving his whip and blowing his horn with his lungs.

"See you later," shouted Jean-Pierre. "We're all going up to the Alpe today, and we'll stay there all summer long!"

"See you soon," replied Thomas, who was busy pushing his goats in the right direction.

Little Robert clapped his hands and shouted:

"See you soon, goats! See you soon!"

The four pairs of eyes fascinated by the agility of the horned beasts shone in the morning light. Heidi had entered the room so softly that the children hadn't heard her. Her heart was pounding as she looked at the four little ones leaning out of the window, barefoot, in their long nightgowns. The joy radiated on her face.

"My little ones!" she murmured. "My own little ones, mine, for all this beautiful summer!"

In fact, the day before, in the evening as they had gathered together, when the grandmother, the two mothers and Lina were examining how the work would be divided up at the chalet, Annette had said, in a tone that didn't allow for a reply:

"You, Granny, will take care of the children. Cooking, washing and tidying up the rooms, ironing, cleaning up, that's our business."

"You will play your role as a grandmother," Ida added.

"What a sweet part of the task you leave me! If I count correctly, with the baby there will be five of them. Ah! If Henry were with us, that would make seven little odds and ends!"

"The seven little dwarves of the mountain!"

"And you will be their fairy! You will be their Snow White…"

"A well aged Snow White," Heidi had sighed wistfully.

"He who keeps his heart young, doesn't get old," concluded Lina, sententiously.

The grandmother remembered this conversation, contemplating the cute curly heads that stood out against the backdrop of the alpine landscape.

The goats had disappeared at the turn of the shortcut leading to Alpe.

Jean-Pierre suddenly turned around and was the first to see Heidi.

"Oh! Grandma! Hello! How are you here? We didn't hear you come in."

"You are reckless, my little ones! In the morning freshness, bare feet on the floor! In a shirt! At the window! It's good for catching a bad cold! Get dressed quickly and go down to the kitchen to wash up a little. Afterwards we'll have lunch with fresh rolls that Lina has picked up for you!"

"It's not Sunday though!" said Marie, very surprised by this treat.

"No, but it's a day of celebration, of great celebration! And then, when you have had lunch, you will put on your studded shoes and we will leave for the chalet."

This programme was a great success with the children, who were ready in the blink of an eye.

Never has breakfast been so quickly swallowed! The rolls were swallowed; four little noses disappeared into four large bowls of fresh milk. Then the slippers flew into the corner of the room and never before had the big mountain shoes been laced so quickly.

The children escaped from the house and, gathered in the garden in front of the door, they made their calls:

"Mummy, Granny, we're ready!"

"What are you waiting for to leave?"

"We will arrive too late."

Heidi, at the door, tried to moderate this feverish impatience:

"We need time to get dressed. We'll be done soon. Come on, calm down! You're more turbulent than Thomas's goats!"

Annette, arriving at the grandmother's help, called the children to her.

"Listen up! And pay attention carefully to what I have to tell you: you are reasonable enough to understand that Ida and I still have a few small preparations to make before we leave. Paul hasn't yet hitched the cart that has to take the luggage up. Since you are now very wise, here is what I propose to you: you will leave right away…"

At these words, undisciplined like Thomas' goats, the four children rushed to the garden gate. Annette called them back in a short order:

"Ah, no! My little friends! Not like that! Listen up! Granny Heidi will ride with you, or rather, you'll ride with grandma. You know she can't run as fast as you can."

Then you will take care of her, on the way and also at the chalet, while waiting for our arrival. I entrust her to you.

"I'll hold her hand," said Jean-Pierre seriously.

"Me too," said little Robert.

"This is good," said Annette, radiant; "and you, Jacqueline and Marie, will walk ahead, don't be too fast."

The children hugged Annette and Ida and quietly set off in the agreed order.

In the meadows, primroses, violets and periwinkle smiled at the small troop. Higher up were the white and mauve crocuses, with a heart of gold, and then the snowdrops.

On the horizon, the Falknis was raising its aerial peak in the transparent air of this beautiful spring morning.

The children looked after the grandmother in their care. They walked, miraculously silent.

"This day reminds me of another one, already far away," says Heidi, as she climbs the path. "I'm thinking of a five-year-old girl, about Marie's age, whose tired aunt was holding her hand. Like us, they went up to the chalet de l'Alpe."

"The little girl was you, wasn't it, Granny?" asked Jacqueline.

"And the aunt's name was Dete!" said Jean-Pierre.

"That's right! But how did you know?"

"Mama has often told us the story of your arrival at the Oncle de l'Alpe."

"Was Uncle de l'Alpe really bad?" asked Marie.

"He was thought to be a bad man in Dörfli because he lived alone and did not like the men who had done him harm. He was so good to me!"

Robert suddenly says :

"Granny, won't you stop for a moment? Aren't you already tired from the climb?"

"And you, my darling?" replied Heidi, guessing the intention of the little man who had been getting his hand pulled for the last few minutes.

"Oh! Me! A little bit... only a little bit!"

"That's good! Let's sit here on the embankment. I have in my basket the last buns you left on the table earlier; and for each one, a bar of chocolate."

Shouts of joy! Eyes that sparkle, hands that stretch out, they had their morning snack.

After the brief stop, they started walking again. The path was steeper; the nails of the ice shoes screeched on the big stones. The order of the little convoy was broken. They walked in single file. Jean-Pierre, the first one, tireless, jumped from one side of the path to the other, running in the grass, in pursuit of a grasshopper. Jacqueline picked pale anemones or purple dog teeth as she passed by. Marie, with a wand in her hand, whipped an imaginary horse. Alone, little Robert remained quietly with the grandmother, singing a tune he invented for himself, to entertain himself.

Soon they reached the chalet.

Heidi could not hold back a cry of surprise and admiration. She hadn't seen the Alpe house again since the transformations. The chalet was unrecognisable; the annex had almost doubled in size. In front of the door, a beautiful terrace, supported by a stone wall, was surrounded by a fence made of crossed fir branches. At the corner stood a large mast with a brand new red flag with a white cross, a shiny spot on the intensely blue sky.

Peter, the grandfather, had gone up at dawn to open doors and windows and air the house. Standing towards the gate, he waited for Heidi, not without emotion.

"Do you like our old chalet this way?"

"Oh, Peter, you didn't tell me everything! It's a hundred times more beautiful than I had imagined. You've been keeping secrets from me, you and Paul!"

"We wanted to surprise you. And you haven't seen everything yet; let's go in!"

The interior of the chalet had retained its mountain character; however, all sorts of details had made it comfortable and attractive.

The old couple sat in the kitchen. Heidi and Peter, without any need for them to tell each other, were thinking of that distant day when she, as a little girl, had got rid of the heavy clothes she had laid on the pasture and he, a young goatherd, had come down to look for the package. Aunt Dete had given him a brand new penny. A penny! It was fortune!

The old chalet with the disjointed planks was a palace.

"My Peter!"

"My dear Heidi!"

They could say no more, so moved and grateful were they.

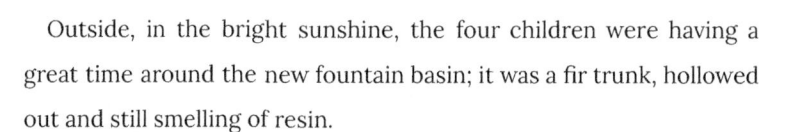

Outside, in the bright sunshine, the four children were having a great time around the new fountain basin; it was a fir trunk, hollowed out and still smelling of resin.

Jean-Pierre cried out:

"Here they are! There they are!"

On the way up the small procession of the other members of the family. Ida and Lina were in the lead; Paul held the horse pulling the carriage by the bridle. On the seat, Annette; the baby was sitting on her lap.

With all the speed of their little legs, the children ran to meet their mothers.

The rest of the morning was spent unpacking the trunks and putting everything in its place.

At lunchtime, Jean-Pierre, proud to show that he knew how to count, noted:

"There are eleven of us at the chalet: Grandpa, Grandma Heidi, Aunt Annette, Mum, Lina, Jacqueline, me, Marie, Robert, the baby, Uncle Paul. When dad will be there on Sunday, there will be twelve of us!"

"What a big family!" says Jacqueline.

"And there is still room around the table!"

"For the ones from America, when they come," says Heidi. "Because I hope they come to visit us soon."

"Who knows? Maybe this year", says Peter.

"What luck! That will make five children, plus cousin Jean and cousin Elizabeth."

"In total: seven!"

"Seven imps in the forest!"

"How much fun we will have!"

After the meal, Heidi took a folder, a bundle of wool and knitting needles and led the children under the three fir trees, which had become majestic tall trees. Their trunks were touching each other at the base and the big roots emerging from the ground formed natural seats. The children sat down around the grandmother; Paul set up a playpen for the baby which Annette delicately brought a few minutes later.

"When there will be seven of us!" exclaimed Jean-Pierre who was pursuing his idea…

"What will you do when there are seven of us?" asked Granny, who guessed the thought of the unruly little one.

"We will play dwarves…"

"Just like in the story of Snow White," says Jacqueline.

"Who is she, Snow White?" Marie asked, intrigued.

"She is a princess," says Jean-Pierre; "a pretty princess who died because she ate an apple."

"Me," said Robert, pensive, "I don't want to eat any more apples."

"But no, she's not dead for good. She married the prince," said Jacqueline.

"Who gave him the apple?"

"His mother," says Jacqueline.

"Oh! the naughty mother!" said Marie, tapping her foot. "She wasn't a real mummy!"

"No," replied Jean-Pierre, "she was a witch."

"And… the little dwarves, what did they do?" asked Robert softly.

"They put Snow White in a glass coffin, and they cried, and then the birds of the forest came, and they threw flower petals on the coffin."

"Your whole story is very confusing! You're confusing everything," says Heidi. "You, Jean-Pierre, who seems to know it so well, could tell it to us."

"I'm afraid of getting confused. Jacqueline would say it better than me."

"And you, Grandma, do you know the story of Snow White and the seven little dwarves?" said Jacqueline in reply.

"Of course, and for a long time already!"

"Oh," said the children in chorus, "Granny, tell it; you tell it best."

"It's a very long story. When you know how to read, I will give you the book written by the Grimm brothers, or another beautiful book made especially for small children, with beautiful pictures, and you will be able to know this nice tale in detail. In the meantime, I will tell you about it, before afternoon tea time."

A long time ago, on a beautiful spring day, a little princess was born. Her mother, the Queen, covered her with kisses and whispered: "Snow White! I call you Snow White!" Suddenly she turned pale and died.

The King remarried, marrying a very beautiful, but jealous, ambitious and mean girl. As she wanted to reign alone, she gave poison to her husband, who perished in great suffering.

Several years passed; Snow White grew up and became more beautiful than the Queen. Above all, she was nicer. Jealous, the Queen relegated the little princess to the servants' quarters and forced her to do the most disgusting household chores.

One day, a young Prince, passing by the castle, saw Snow White and found her so beautiful that he decided to marry her. The Queen discovered this secret plan - for she was a witch - and decided to make the princess disappear. She ordered one of her officers to take Snow White, kill her, rip her heart out and bring it back in a magic box. The servant did not dare to carry out his tragic mission; he abandoned Snow White in the forest and put the heart of a doe he had slaughtered into the box.

"It was good for the nasty fake mummy," says Marie.

"What about the little dwarves?" asked Robert.

"Wait for the rest," Heidi says, smiling. "You're in a hurry!"

So Snow White, left alone, went into the forest. Exhausted, she lay down on the ground and fell asleep. A small rabbit, then a squirrel, a doe and her fawns, birds, even a turtle and all the animals of the woods soon surrounded her and looked after her. When she woke up, they took her to a small thatched cottage, lost in the middle of a clearing.

"It was the house of the dwarves," says Jacqueline.

"Of the seven little dwarves," added Jean-Pierre, who loved precision. "Their names were Doc, Sneezy, Happy, Grumpy, Bashful, Sleepy and Dopey…"

"You're a genius," says Heidi. "I would never have remembered all their names."

When Snow White arrived at the home of the dwarves, the dwarves were absent. They had left to work in their mine, from which they extracted gold, clear diamonds and sparkling precious stones. With the help of all the animals, her friends, she cleaned the cottage, washed the dishes and tidied up the place. Then she prepared the soup.

Think about the surprise of the little dwarves when they return! At first, they were suspicious of the new arrival and held a council to decide whether to keep her or whether to drive her away.

"They kept her, didn't they, Granny," Robert asked anxiously.

"Of course they kept her with them. She was so nice and knew how to bake such good pies!"

At that moment Annette came out of the chalet and clapped her hands and shouted:

"Come quickly, afternoon tea is waiting for you."

"Oh! Not yet," begged Marie, "quickly tell us the end of the story ... then we'll go and have afternoon tea afterwards."

"No, my children! We must obey your mother! Come along! But..." said Heidi suddenly, "where has Jean-Pierre disappeared to?"

Jacqueline chuckled. The grandmother was worried:

"He was there five minutes ago and he hasn't come back to the chalet, I would have seen him."

"Maybe it's the little dwarves who took him away!" says Jacqueline mischievously.

"Or the birds," Marie added.

"Or the little squirrel," Robert continued.

In his playpen, the baby was stamping his feet, reaching up to the top of the highest of the three fir trees and making little chuckles of joy. At that moment a dry cone fell at Heidi's feet. Everyone raised their heads and saw Jean-Pierre on one of the highest branches of the tree.

"You see, Granny, I was right, it was a squirrel that took him away!" says Robert triumphantly.

Heidi, anxious, called:

"Jean-Pierre, my boy. You are too reckless. Will you please come down! Go slowly. You're scaring me. Naughty little squirrel. Watch out! Behave yourself! This branch is not strong. Take the other one, the one on the right. There!"

Jean-Pierre, as agile as a monkey, was very quickly at the foot of his perch. Heidi, trembling, took him in her arms.

"My darling, don't climb up the trees anymore! Don't scare me like that anymore! An accident happens so quickly. You could have broken your arms and legs if you had fallen. Promise me you won't do it again."

"Oh, yes! I promise," said the boy, saddened to have put his dear Granny in such a state. "I won't climb any more trees... at least not when I'm with you," he added in a quiet voice, as if speaking to himself.

We went for a snack. Annette scolded her son very loudly because of his daring ascent.

After drinking their cups of milk and devouring their honey toast, the children dragged the grandmother back under the trees and she had to tell them the end of the story of Snow White.

Heidi told them how the wicked Queen had discovered the deception of her servant and how, disguised as a beggar, she went to the cottage of the little dwarves, where Snow White, unsuspecting, having bitten the poisoned apple, immediately fell to the ground.

*The little dwarves found her lying on the floor. She only seemed to be asleep. When they could not revive her, they laid her down in a coffin shining with gold and crystal. They carried the coffin to a clearing and took turns watching her.*

*A year later, the Prince finally discovered the coffin and, leaning over it, put his lips on it. The Queen Witch's charm was broken. Snow White woke up, smiled and rode on the Prince's horse to the Castle of Dreams with him. The Prince married Snow White and they lived happily ever after.*

"And the wicked Queen, what has become of her?" asked Marie.

"She had been chased by the dwarves and all the animals of the forest; she was struck by lightning as she clung to a large rock and fell into the precipice. She was never seen again."

"What about the little dwarves? asked Robert."

"They were very happy with their friend's happiness; they continued to sing while working in their mine… where they may still be today. "

"On that note," says Heidi, "let's go for a little walk together in the pasture before supper."

The story of Snow White had made a big impression on the children. And all night long the four children dreamt about Snow White, the seven little dwarfs and the wicked witch.

# CHAPTER NINE

## GOOD NEWS

There had not been such a beautiful June for many years. The pastures were enamelled with thousands of multicoloured flowers which raised their corollas above the grass, so thick and filling the air with their subtle scent. The sun illuminated the Scesaplana glacier under a cloudless sky and at sunset the rocks of the Alps were tinged with purple while a light wind rushed through the fir-tops.

Peter, with the help of his son Paul, had always cultivated the most beautiful flowers in his garden or in his greenhouses in Dörfli, but around the cottage he had surpassed himself. On a small rocky outcrop, tufts of cyclamen, daphnes, a few vanilla orchids, brooms and cytises spread a delicious scent. Holly was growing in the shade of the fir trees. The children called this intimate place, where they spent such beautiful hours listening to the stories told by grandmother, the "green room". Grandfather Pierre had built three small benches, made of stakes planted in the ground, on which he had nailed planks of roughly planed larch wood.

Every day, the household was up early. For the children would not have wanted to miss the fun spectacle of the goats on the mountain pasture for anything in the world.

Thomas, the goatherd, announced his arrival from far away, blowing as hard as he could in his little horn. Usually, he didn't stop, just greeting everybody on the way.

That morning, contrary to his habit, he overtook the unruly troop of his unruly animals and in three jumps he was at the door of the chalet. He was holding a letter in his hand and handed it to Heidi, shouting: "Here is news from America!"

He did not have the opportunity to say more. The letter had the same effect on the family as a pebble thrown at an anthill! In a second, the grandmother was assaulted by the children, by the mothers, by Lina and by Paul. The grandfather took the envelope and, without haste, as befits the head of the family, opened it with the blade of his military knife.

"Read the letter, Grandpa," the children shouted, jumping like goats. "Read it quickly!"

This din had scattered the herd of horned and bearded quadrupeds; Thomas had a hard time gathering them all together and getting them back on the road. The whole family went to the "green living room" still wet with dew; Grandma Heidi read the message.

"New York, May 25, 1939.

Dear all of you,

These lines will surely reach you at the Chalet de l'Alpe. They bring you good news that will give you as much pleasure as it gives us to tell you: in a month's time, all four of us will be heading towards you, to Switzerland.

The manager of the factory where I work wants to take advantage of the Swiss National Exhibition in Zurich to do business with various houses in our country. I'm delighted that he will be able to take me along with him, as I think I can be of use to him in his dealings.

That's not all: he will pay for the trip for my whole family and even give us a holiday until September.

As we will have to stop in London and then Paris, we only expect to reach Zurich in the first few days of July.

I will inform you of the exact date of our arrival as soon as we are in Europe."

"What happy news!" exclaimed Heidi, interrupting the reading.

"All together, for two months; yahoo!" launched Jean-Pierre into the luminous morning air.

And the echo of the rock answered "Yoo-hoo!"

"Go on with your reading," said Annette, curious.

"I don't think the children are interested in what follows," said Heidi, quickly going through the other six typed pages. "We'll read it quietly, one at a time; let's go and have lunch."

What a cheerful chirping brightened up the meal that morning! The little birds in the branches of a cherry blossom tree made no more noise at sunrise than did the children in the chalet, commenting on the news. The baby himself had understood that a great event was brewing: he was shouting and hitting his big bowl with his little spoon, at the risk of breaking it.

Grandfather had read the letter to the end.

"There are some details in there," he says, pointing to the sheets of paper, "that interest all of you, especially the children: Henry will come to Europe with his car."

How?" said Robert. He crosses the sea by car?

"Half-wit!" replied Jean-Pierre. "He is crossing the Ocean in a liner; he will put his car on the boat. All Americans do that when they come to Europe."

"Uncle Henry is not an American," replied Jacqueline, "he's Swiss!"

"Shall we go in his car?" Marie asked shyly, wiping her lips smeared with redcurrant jam.

"You know very well that motorists can't come to Dörfli; it's forbidden!" says Jean-Pierre with a superior air.

"Then we'll go to Zurich!" says Jacqueline.

"You're not seriously thinking about it, my little one," replied Annette.

"That's where you're wrong, Grandma," said the grandfather. "Henry, a little further on, suggested that we meet in Zurich. We will visit the Exhibition together and all of us will return to the Chalet de l'Alpe to spend the summer there. The parents will take the train and Uncle Henry will drive all the children to Maienfeld, where he will leave his car in a garage."

What mad cheerfulness took hold of the children.

"Are there any other surprises in the letter? Asked Marie.

"So they will also stay at the chalet, Uncle Henry, Aunt Edith, Cousin Jean, Cousin Elizabeth! What luck!" enthused Robert.

"It will seem funny to them, who live in a big 28-storey house!" says Jacqueline, dreamy.

"Wrong, my little one," said grandfather. "A few weeks ago Henry left his skyscraper, as they say over there. He has had a country house built, far from the town, which, he says in the letter, looks like the "Manoir House". He even called it by a pretty name reminiscent of Dörfli: "Rose de l'Alpe" (Rose of the Alpe). This has only one disadvantage for him: he can no longer go home every day. He only goes home to his wife and children on Sundays."

"Just like daddy," Jean-Pierre remarked; he only comes up from Maienfeld on Sundays, when we are at the chalet!

At the beginning of the afternoon, as was the custom on the first day, Heidi, surrounded by the children, rested in the "green lounge".

A lively conversation ensued about "the Americans".

"How old is Cousin Jean?"

"Twelve years old."

"And cousin Elizabeth?"

"Nine years old."

"They are older than us! Do you think they will want to have fun with us?"

"Are there mountains in New York?"

"No, my little ones. New York is a huge city, as big as the space that stretches from Dörfli to Ragaz."

"And there is nothing but houses? There are no pastures, no forests?"

"Nothing but tall houses, 28 storeys high."

"Are the houses made of wood, like our chalet?"

"No, in stone, like the "Manoir House", like our school, like our church."

"It is sad, the stone, if there are no trees around."

"Fortunately, they now live in the countryside."

"In the countryside there are meadows, flowers, trees and birds."

"However, in New York there are no mountains, no great forests, no shining glaciers."

"The sun must be very annoyed not to be able to gild rock faces when it sets."

"Nor when it gets up…"

"Uncle Henry once wrote that the sun rose in the sea."

"Is it all wet then?" Marie asked.

They all started out laughing.

""Rose de l'Alpe", said Jacqueline, dreaming. ""Rose de l'Alpe" is a pretty name for a house in America."

"The "Manoir" is also a nice name."

"Tell us, Granny, what's the name of our chalet?"

"It has no name. It's curious, but that's the way it is. We call it 'the chalet' quite simply," Heidi replied, surprised herself. No one has ever given it another name; it used to be Uncle's cottage. Since Uncle died we have been saying: the chalet de l'Alpe."

"There are many other "Alpine chalets" above Dörfli, and elsewhere too, and everywhere."

"I," said Jean-Pierre, "would like it to have a name too. What if we called it 'Flower of America'? Uncle Henry called his American house "Rose de l'Alpe"; why shouldn't our Swiss house be called "Fleur d'Amérique"?"

"I don't know if grandpa would like that very much," says Heidi with a smile. Let's look for something better."

The children's imagination could give free rein to their imagination in this brand new game: looking for a name for the chalet. Silence prevails for a few minutes, as if it were a riddle. In short, it wasn't a riddle; it was much more difficult.

"Why don't we call it "Bouby"?"

"Or "Elizabeth"; there is a beautiful house in Maienfeld called "Villa Elizabeth"!"

"Or "Jean"?"

"Oh no! "Jean" is not a good name for a Swiss chalet."

"I've got it," says Marie, clapping her hands, as if to applaud her idea: "Grandma Heidi! That will please Grandpa!"

"You're very nice, cute," said the grandmother. I'd still prefer something else... A flower name, for example, but not your "Flower of America", my friend Jean-Pierre! Or a mountain name. Let's look for something better."

Proposals were put forward, names were jostled in a cascade:

"The Falknis!"

"The Golden Teeth!"

"Primrose!"

"Daffodil!"

"Periwinkle!"

"Violet!"

"Snowdrop! I want it to be called 'Snowdrop'," Jacqueline cried with authority. "It will remind us of the beautiful legend that Grandma has so often told us."

" 'Snowdrop' is nice; it's fresh; I like Snowdrop very much," Heidi agreed.

We were about to adopt - "Snowdrop", when Marie, holding her little finger up to the sky, inspired by an easy to understand association of ideas, proposed:

" 'Snow White' ?"

It was a find! Snow White! The chalet "Snow White"! These two words contained so many things:

Quite a nice story: the little princess, the seven little dwarfs, Doc Sneezy, Dopey and the others, and then the golden and crystal coffin, and also the rabbits, the squirrels, the birds of the deep forest! And the beautiful Prince who woke up the Princess... And also the little thatched cottage.

"And those who don't understand, says Jean-Pierre, will believe that the chalet is called so because of the real snow, the thick white snow that covers the whole Alps in winter."

As a sign of approval, he kissed Marie on both cheeks and then jumped on grandma Heidi's neck.

"Long live "Snow White". Let's go and see what grandpa thinks about it!"

"He will certainly be delighted."

The grandfather approved the proposal of the "Council of Little Dwarves" without any difficulty.

The children had no respite until they informed Annette, Ida and Lina. They walked in single file through the whole chalet, the hall, the dining room, the kitchen, the bedrooms, the stable and the hayloft, singing to a rhythmic melody they had just invented:

"Snow White, the Snow White Chalet!"

"Snow White, long live Snow White!"

Accompanied by Heidi, they even went to meet Thomas and the goats to tell them the news.

The goatherd came down that evening with a large bouquet of splendid red flowers in his hand: the first rhododendrons of the year.

"Take these flowers for you and for the chalet."

"Flowers for 'Snow White'," said the children's choir.

"Where did you pick them?" asked Jean-Pierre.

"Up there, on the Rocher de l'Aigle (Eagle Rock)," replied the goatherd, pointing to the enormous steep wall.

"I want to go and pick some, too! Are there many of them?"

"Whole bushes! Farewell, Jean-Pierre, I have to catch up with my goats."

Thomas cracked his whip, blew into his horn and hurried down the path in great strides.

## CHAPTER TEN

## A DAY OF ANGUISH AT 'BLANCHE NEIGE' (SNOW WHITE)

The following day was a Sunday, and Uncle Claude had come up from Maienfeld. At the time when everyone used to rest in the chalet, Heidi, with her work basket hanging from her arm, went to the "green living room" to knit. She sat down quietly on her folding chair and prepared her woollen bundle and needles. Jean-Pierre stood in front of her and began to talk to her in great detail about a bush covered with red flowers that sparkled among the larches, towards Rocher de l'Aigle. His eyes opened wide and bright. The more he talked about it, the more he saw the attractive bush in his imagination and the more it came to life. Jacqueline was looking at the illustrations in a book of legends. Robert and Marie, sitting on the moss, were teasing a large, brown, hairy caterpillar with a twig.

Heidi put her basket down on the ground and said :

"Sit down now, Jean-Pierre, and keep quiet. We will all go together one of these next days to contemplate this beautiful bush."

But Jean-Pierre did not obey.

"I have to go and see my grandfather quickly, I have a lot to tell him," he said as he headed towards the chalet.

After a while, as the child did not reappear, Heidi said to Jacqueline:

"I think grandfather has already gone for a walk with your father. Go and get your brother, so that he doesn't wake up your mother who is resting."

Jacqueline ran to the chalet, but she didn't come back for a long time. Then Heidi got up and went to see what was going on. There was silence everywhere. There was no one in the dining room. In the kitchen, where Ida and Lina wiped the dishes while chatting, Jean-Pierre hadn't appeared. She went up the little staircase and entered the children's room: it was empty. Through the open front door, she saw Annette sleeping. She went downstairs and met Jacqueline coming back from the goat stable. She had looked everywhere for her brother, but she hadn't found him anywhere. Heidi was beginning to worry.

"Oh! Why did I not call back Jean-Pierre right away?" she repeated in a low voice.

What was to be done? Where to look for the child? Wouldn't he have escaped to run to the foot of the rocks to see where the eagles were sleeping? Wouldn't he have gone further up, towards the larch trees, to pick the flowers he was talking about so enthusiastically earlier? Who knows if he had not wanted to join the goatherd with whom he had been seen talking the day before? The more Heidi thought, the more worried she became.

She thought that someone should be sent to the goat herd immediately before telling Annette about it. Paul arrived on these premises. He decided to go up to the pasture and promised to come down as soon as possible.

Heidi firmly expected Paul to return with the child; but it was a long wait; long before her brother returned, Annette came down from her room. She had to be told everything. The poor distraught mother wanted to go anywhere in search of her child.

However, Heidi was so convinced that Jean-Pierre had run away to visit the goatherd that she ended up appeasing Annette while waiting for the return of the fugitive. To tell the truth, she was not very reassured. She went from one window to the other, appeared on the threshold of the door, scanned the horizon or went around the chalet, returned to sit down towards the little ones. Finally Paul arrived, out of breath; he was alone. Thomas, the goatherd, had not seen the child. Annette burst into tears; Ida and Lina were dismayed.

"If only Peter and Claude were here!" Heidi kept repeating over and over again. "What should we do?"

In the meantime, by a happy coincidence, the grandfather and Claude returned from their short walk. Heidi and Annette explained to them in a few words what had happened. Claude advised them not to panic and to stay put while the grandfather, Paul and himself took the necessary steps to find the child.

Peter set off to explore the heights and the neighbouring rocks, while Claude went towards the forest to search it in all directions; Paul went towards the stream.

Heidi and the three anxious young women could hear the hours and half hours ringing one after the other on the old clock in the dining room. The afternoon had never seemed so long to them. At the slightest noise in the distance, they would jump to their feet and say: "they've brought the child back."

Thus passed a time that seemed like centuries. The four women, exhausted with anguish and grief, would occasionally let out a deep sigh from their chest or a tear from their eyelids.

With her hands clasped in her lap, Heidi prayed...

Three hours later, Pierre and Claude arrived together, very pale.

"Are you bringing back my Jean-Pierre?" shouted Annette, who for a moment hadn't been able to stay still.

"Alas!" said Peter, "I looked everywhere near the rocks and I saw nothing anywhere."

"I," moans Claude, "walked through the forest in every different direction, it's not possible for our child to be there."

Paul returned too, without bringing back any reassuring news.

At that moment, Thomas the goatherd was coming down from the pasture with his herd.

"I've been thinking," he said as he approached Paul, "and I think I know where the little boy is."

"You mustn't talk for nothing," Claude reproached him, annoyed. "How could you know since you were up there all day with your goats and you didn't see him?" Thomas repeated halfway through:

"Yet I know where he is."

Claude took the goatherd by the hand and told him more calmly :

"Take a good look at me, my boy, and answer. Do you really know anything about my son?"

"Yes," Thomas said again.

"So talk fast! Where did he go?"

"I'll take you there right away if grandfather wants to keep my goats."

"I will take care of it; go quickly, my sons, and may God have you in His holy care!"

Thomas walked through meadows towards the gorge where the stream was. The two men followed him. He continued on his way without letting himself be stopped by brush or thorns. When he reached a clearing where several large rhododendrons were blooming, he stopped and looked around in disbelief. He had expected to find Jean-Pierre there. However, he set off again with the same confident step. The flowering bushes were becoming rarer and rarer, but bigger and bigger. In front of each of them the goatherd stopped for a moment, nodded his head and started on his way again.

"No, Thomas! Don't go any further," Paul suddenly shouted to him. "This way we come directly to the rock walls of the stream."

At that moment a burning bush was seen between the fir trees. The setting sun lit up huge clumps of flowers in a brilliant red. Thomas turned around and repeated several times:

"He's here! He's here!"

Claude and Paul made a single leap. The goatherd's premonitions had led him to the right place. Barely one metre from the precipice, Jean-Pierre was asleep on the grass, a big bunch in his arms. His breathing was irregular and he seemed very agitated. Claude kissed him on the forehead; he called him gently: "Jean-Pierre ... Jean-Pierre." The child opened his eyes and whispered half asleep:

"The fairies! Snow White! The prince! The witch! Let go of me!"

He woke up completely, sat down and rubbed his eyes:

"Daddy! Uncle Paul! Thomas! I'm glad you've come for me. I was dreaming about the ugly witch who wanted to take me with her to the bottom of Rocher de l'Aigle." He put his arms around the neck of his father and his uncle kneeling next to him, in the grip of strong emotion.

"Let's not waste a minute! Let's go straight away to reassure mother, Granma Heidi and Aunt Ida who are lamenting and think that you are lost," ordered Claude, dragging his son by the hand. Paul and Thomas followed them. While walking as fast as he could, Claude questioned the goatherd.

"Thomas, tell me," he asked, "how did you know that our boy had wandered away, near the bushes where we fortunately found him?"

"He told me yesterday that he absolutely wanted to pick a bouquet of red flowers," replied the goatherd.

"Yes, but what gave you the idea to look in the direction of the rocks of the stream?"

"Since he wasn't at the first bush, it was proof that he had gone further, because I know that the further you go, the more beautiful the flowers become and that in the end the most beautiful bush is at the edge of the rock that hangs over the precipice."

They were soon no longer far from "Snow White" where the goats were frolicking under Pierre's guard.

Thomas blew joyfully into his cornet and called "yu-chee"s into the valley. Heidi and Annette set off to meet the group, followed by the goats that had recognised the call of their herdsman.

"There's the four of them! Praise the Lord! My Jean-Pierre! My little Jean-Pierre," shouted Annette, crying with joy.

She pressed her child against her, while tears flooded her face.

"My Jean-Pierre! Why did you go all alone, so far away? Why didn't you come back faster? Naughty darling!"

"He had fallen asleep on the grass with a bouquet in his arms," Claude said.

Jean-Pierre, freed from his Grandma's embrace, didn't know what to take: he expected to be scolded very loudly:

"There you go, Granny," he says, regaining confidence. "These beautiful flowers are for you."

"Goodbye," says Thomas; "I'm very late with my goats. I am leaving."

Indeed, the shadow had already spread over the valley. The peaks were wonderfully illuminated by the last rays of the sun.

"Goodbye, Thomas, welcome back, and thank you from the bottom of my heart," shouted Heidi, as the goatherd hurriedly descended with his herd to Mayenfeld.

"We will never forget the service you have done us," added Jean-Pierre's mother.

***

A few days later, Claude, the doctor in Maienfeld, gave the goatherd's mother an envelope containing a hundred franc note with these words:

"On behalf of Jean-Pierre's grateful family."

## CHAPTER ELEVEN

## AT THE EXHIBITION

The big day was approaching. Grandma Heidi had her hands full answering the questions the children were asking her.

All the details of the trip - a real expedition! - had been checked; baby Bouby, although he was now able to walk on his own, would stay in "Snow White" with Lina. Jean-Pierre, Jacqueline, Marie and Robert would go down the day before, on a Tuesday, with Grandma and mother, to sleep in Maienfeld at Uncle Claude's house. Grandfather, Uncle Paul and Aunt Ida would join them on Wednesday morning when the train left.

"I," said Jean-Pierre, "shall take my whip."

"And I, my whistle and my hoop," added Robert.

"And I, my doll Lisy," continued Marie.

"Don't even think about it," Heidi cried, "you shouldn't burden yourself with bulky items. They will bother you all day long. You'll have so many beautiful things to see that you won't have time to enjoy yourself."

"Are there lions at the Exhibition?" asked Jacqueline. "I'd like so much to see real, living lions."

"Certainly not," replied Grandma bursting out laughing, "this is not a menagerie!"

"Will we take a boat trip?"

"I'm looking forward to seeing the machines…"

"I want to see an aeroplane…"

"Is it true that there is a real Swiss village?"

"Yes, my little Marie, and it is even called "Dörfli" like our village," Heidi replied.

Heidi had read many newspaper articles and had obtained the plan of the Zurich Exhibition. She already knew everything that might be of interest to the children of "Snow White"; she wondered, however, whether Jean and Elizabeth would share their enthusiasm. The two grandchildren of America were not jaded? Well, they are also 12 and 9 year olds! It could be handled on the spot when it happened.

A few more days went by, filled with beautiful walks. On the way, they talked often about visiting the exhibition and the "Landi" as it was known throughout the German-speaking part of Switzerland.

Finally, the much talked about Tuesday arrived and they went down to Maienfeld. Not much sleeping happened that night in doctor Claude's house!

Already by seven o'clock in the morning, the whole family was gathered on the platform of the small railway station. They climbed into a carriage three-quarters full of travellers who were also travelling to Zurich.

So many discoveries to be made, from the windows of the express train that took them away at full speed! The castle of Sargans, straight on its high rock, passed in a vision as fast as lightning. And then at a walking pace along the narrow Walenstadt lake, dominated on the other side by a jagged mountain range even more impressive than the walls of the Falknis. Short tunnels, which were crossed in a thunderous roar, brought the children to the height of their joy. A moment later, we approached Lake Zurich. The track passed so close to the water that the train seemed to run on the waves. Tall, white steamboats sailed between the two shores.

The little family was very excited. The ticket inspector passed in the wagon announcing "Zurich!". The children clapped their hands and rushed to the window to get a better view of the big city.

Jean-Pierre, the first, saw the sharp spires of the cathedral and discovered two pylons standing on each of the quays of the harbour:

"The two towers of the "Landi" cable car!" he exclaimed, triumphant. "I recognize them! That's it! Here we are! Hurrah!"

The train slowed down; slowly entered the station and stopped.

The large glass hall and the swarming mass of travellers made the Dörfli mountain dwellers dizzy, as they had never been in such a rush before.

Grandma Heidi was a little nervous: firstly, because she was afraid of losing one of the children in the crowd, and secondly, because her heart was beating with the thought that in a few minutes she would see her son Henry again. They had arranged to meet at the second class buffet.

To make sure they didn't get lost, the children held hands tightly; Robert walked behind his Granny whom he had grabbed by the skirt.

Not without difficulty, they made their way through. Heidi was deeply moved when she hugged her oldest son Henry, who had become a real gentleman, in her heart. The fourteen members of Heidi's family took turns kissing each other with enthusiastic and touching greetings, without worrying about the customers at the neighbouring tables. This went on for a while.

"That's not all," says Henry, a practical man; "if we want to see the essentials of the Exhibition, we mustn't waste time. Here's what I've combined: there's no question of using the buses to get to the 'Landi', they're taken by storm and you get run over, just like in the trams, by the way. I parked my car nearby. I will make a first trip with grandma and the children, then two more transports and in half an hour we will all be together at the entrance of the "Haute Route". (High Road)"

"The one with all the flags?" asked Jean-Pierre.

"You seem well informed, my nephew!" said Uncle Henry. "My little man, I am going to make you happy: you'll sit next to me, in the front seat of the car."

"How nice you are! Uncle Henry! Let's go quickly. Goodbye everyone! See you later!"

The heavy traffic that reigned that day in no way intimidated the driving uncle, used to playing with all obstacles in the streets of New York.

Jean-Pierre, amazed, admired the skill with which his uncle operated the levers, buttons and all the instruments. He saw nothing of the street!

Behind him, Jean and Elizabeth were explaining to their cousins Marie and Jacqueline, their cousin Robert and also to Grandma Heidi all that could be seen in the beautifully paved Rue de la Gare. They had been in Zurich for a week and were able to point out in passing the smallest details in the many toy, clothing and stationery shop windows in this artery.

"But," Jean hastened to add, "you know, in New York, houses are ten times higher, streets are five times wider; and then you drive on the left. Dad had a hard time getting used to keeping to his right, in Paris and Switzerland."

The entrance to the Exhibition was impressive: huge banners in the colours of the Swiss cantons floated in the morning breeze and joyfully greeted the new arrivals.

On the first bridge of the "Haute Route", also known as the "chemin de ronde" (walkway), 3,000 flags with the coats of arms of Switzerland's 3,000 municipalities formed a multicoloured ceiling.

Uncle Henry, who had studied all the stands in detail, drew up the programme for the day.

"You can't see everything in one day! There are too many of them. So we will divide ourselves into two groups: Betty will lead the parents towards what interests them most, the pavilions of fashion, textile industries, furniture, watchmaking and jewellery, etc., and me, I will lead the children with their grandmother to places which will certainly please them much more. At half past twelve, we will all meet at the small landing stage and go to the other side for lunch."

Everyone could only agree with this proposal, even Heidi, who realised that the plan she had drawn up in Dörfli proved to be insufficient.

And they parted.

The children didn't have enough eyes to see all these accumulated wonders. The smallest detail caught their attention. They didn't understand everything, but they were ecstatic everywhere and it took all the diplomatic persuasion of Heidi and Henry to pull them away from contemplating the engravings and the curious armies of little wooden men ingeniously depicted in statistical tables.

Upon leaving the "Haute Route" - it was after ten o'clock - Uncle Henry, who had planned everything, gathered the six children together and said to them:

"I am sure you are thirsty and hungry; am I right?"

"Yes, yes", they answered together.

"The food stand is nearby," Jean, who had a good memory, remarked wisely.

"Well! Let's go," said Heidi, who wasn't mad either, to rest for a moment and have a little snack.

"You'll see how chic it is," says Elizabeth, taking Jacqueline along; "there's everything we want: cheese, rolls, sausages, cakes, soup, biscuits, lemonade, cider; you just have to choose."

Indeed, countless counters offered their victuals at a good price. If all their desires had been satisfied, the grandchildren and Grandma Heidi would have suffered a lot of indigestion! Uncle Henry decided that everyone would be entitled to one of those big white buns called "balloons" and a dish of his or her choice.

Jean did not hesitate: "I would like a sausage!"

Elizabeth chose a small cheese; Jean-Pierre asked for a large slice of ham, Jacqueline for a ration of galantine; Robert for a redcurrant tart covered with cream, which he smeared on the tip of his nose, cheeks and hands. There were drinks of cider or lemonade, or orange syrup.

While the children were enjoying their meal, Uncle Henry lit his pipe, straight and short. "A pipe from America" declared Jean-Pierre, with his mouth full.

For a moment Robert had only been paying attention to a small road train that was running on the main roads. He approached his grandmother who had sat in an aluminium armchair and whispered in his ear

"Say, Grandma, are we going to go, too, into the little train? Tell Uncle Henry; I don't dare. I would like to."

"I guess I'm granting your wish," intervened the uncle. "Well yes, rejoice; we are going for a ride in the little train."

This promise had an immediate effect: the last bite was swallowed in a hurry, the last drop drunk and the small herd went to the starting station. Imagine miniature wagons, uncovered, pulled by an electric locomotive, with everyone sitting there in the direction of travel. Eight people in the cart were enough to fill it; there was a violent rush to take one. It was the most beautiful trip one could make, a fairy-tale journey. The buildings of the "Landi", clear and attractive, lined both sides of the street.

Jean, very proud of his knowledge, pointed out the houses in passing.

"On the right is the model hotel. It's like a real hotel, with beds, bathrooms, balconies, flowers. Here is the rubber palace; you can see how tyres for bicycles and cars are made, and also footballs. This is chemistry; there are big tubes and huge glass balls; dad says it's very interesting; I didn't understand anything about it. This is sports, and next to it, the army. Daddy, daddy ! Let's go down to see the skis and the cannons."

The convoy stopped there. Down they went and the six little ones, very excited, rushed into the army stand. Jean led them without hesitation towards the beautiful cannon which it was not forbidden to touch! He wielded the breech and explained how it worked.

"Does it kill enemies?" asked Marie.

"Of course, and every time, 18 kilometres away!" says Jean.

"It's far, 18 kilometres?" said Robert.

"Very far away, as far as there," says Jean-Pierre, pointing to the mountains at the other end of the lake.

"So," asked Jacqueline, "how is it done, since you can't see the enemies that far away??"

"We calculate!" Jean replied confidently.

"Bravo! You'll be a good gunner, my little one", a soldier in a helmet, watching over the room, couldn't help but exclaim.

Jean, with pleasure, became as red as the soldier's facings.

Then everyone wanted to enter the cockpit of the splendid plane lying on the lawn. With the help of their imagination, they saw themselves, in turn, carried away into the air, high, much higher than the Falknis, much higher than the clouds.

Then on to the sports pavilion. What wonders! The skis especially left them dreaming. In Dörfli, as in New York, they had never had the opportunity to see them so closely! Jean-Pierre said that the postman in Dörfli owned a pair, but he had never seen him use them.

The children discussed among themselves and free-spirited, promised to tell their parents about it. In winter, when there would be a lot of snow in Dörfli, one could use these long boards for walking. Why not them too? They knew that the children from Davos and St. Moritz went on skis... It should be talked about when the time comes.

"Why not you too?" said Uncle Henry, who was listening to their conversation. "You're right: we'll talk about it again. And now I have a nice surprise in store for you. Follow me..."

They passed under one of the bridges of the "Haute-Route". Between two fresh lawns, filled with magnificent flowers, the path went up to a small wooded hill. At the end of an esplanade, a real mountain, on a small scale. A railway line made long curves, crossed viaducts and went into tunnels. In the foreground, a wide plain, partly covered by a forest with tiny trees, a small blue lake and, on both sides of a white road, chalets, such as those at Dörfli, like "Snow White". Running on the track there was a train climbing up, a faithful reproduction of the one that transports travellers from Bern - to Brig.

Uncle Henri explained:

"It is an exact reproduction of the Lötschberg massif and the railway that runs through it; a work of art of which our country's engineers can be proud!"

"Are the real tunnels and bridges far from Zurich?" asked Jean-Pierre.

"Relatively yes, we couldn't go today," Henry replied with a smile.

"And Dörfli?"

"So far away! When you are older, you will certainly make this beautiful journey."

"Say, Uncle Henry, in America, are there big bridges like these too?"

"There are also, and much longer ones."

"Oh, that's a pity!" said Jean-Pierre, a little disappointed in his national self-esteem.

"Console yourself and be proud, my little one. The most beautiful and boldest, a suspension bridge, was built in San-Francisco by one, Swiss, one of our compatriots named Ammann."

"There is a baker in Maienfeld called Ammann! Perhaps he is a relative of the man who built the bridge to America," exclaimed Jacqueline, happy to be able to make this connection."

"It's possible," says Uncle Henry. "The bridge I'm talking about has a beautiful name: the Golden Gate Bridge!"

"Did you pass it, uncle?" asked little Robert.

"Yes, last year, by car, with Aunt Edith, Jean and Elizabeth."

Robert looked with admiration at his uncle and then at his cousin, who had crossed the Golden Gate bridge!

A new surprise had to be promised to pull the children away from contemplating the little Lötschberg train, which ran so fast and so well on its Alpine route.

Down the hill of the park they went to arrive very close to a canal on which multicoloured boats in the shape of a crate sailed one behind the other at a short distance!

Only six people could take a seat in one of these strange zesty boats. Uncle Henry, to Grandma's horror, boldly allowed the six children to be alone in a boat. He himself got into the next one with Grandma.

The "Enchanted River" had a weak current, so well-calculated that one could glide quietly under the flowering trees or through several exhibition halls. Gigantic machines made of polished steel were at eye level, and then, in the middle of a flower bed, statues followed by large, strangely shaped chemical apparatus.

Suddenly they passed under a small bridge with sloping ramps. It was only a cry in the children's boat:

"Grandma! Grandpa! Aunt Edith! Uncle Paul! Papa!"

At the top of the little bridge, by a surprising coincidence, the parents gathered together watched the boats pass by and were for a moment all worried to see their turbulent youngsters alone on the Enchanted River!

"Be good!"

"So stay calm!"

"Where is Grandma?"

In the next boat, the grandmother and her son laughed in the amazement of the parents leaning over the fence. They in turn passed under the bridge and Henry cast to the reassured family

"Admire your daring navigators and don't miss out!"

With regret the children had to leave their beautiful "ship".

At the appointed time, the whole family got on board one of the cute "flies" which constantly shuttled from one shore of the lake to the other.

On the terrace of a beautiful restaurant built on stilts, a good meal was enjoyed by alll. The conversations were extremely lively, laughter was flowing at the end of the table where the children were gathered, enthusiastic about their morning.

However, without a doubt, the happiest person at the table was grandmother Heidi. Together, her radiant face betrayed the joy she felt to be in the midst of all her children and grandchildren. And in her heart she blessed God for giving her the opportunity to live this day.

"When we are all in Dörfli, at home, it will be even more beautiful!" said Heidi

"Tomorrow evening," says Annette, "we will possess this great happiness."

"Tomorrow evening..." Heidi murmured.

After the meal, Henry announced:

"We still have three hours left before we leave the Exhibition. I am sure that parents will find it interesting to visit the "Dörfli" of the "Landi", whose varied architecture represents the various regions of our country, with its small farm, its model farm which houses valuable livestock; there are the most instructive stands for mountain dwellers: arboriculture, market gardening, dairy industry, etc., etc. As for me, I'm taking grandmother and the children along again. At five o'clock we will all meet up at the Riesbach exit gate at the foot of the cable car tower."

Uncle Henry, who had decidedly prepared the day in great detail, took the children to the attractions just a few steps from the restaurant. A strange robot, a sort of metal mechanic in the shape of a man, which walked by itself, frightened Marie and Robert very much, who hid behind their Granny's skirt, while it intrigued and interested the two big boys to the utmost.

A little further on, there was a lot of fun to be had in front of curious dolls, big and small, dressed in the national costumes of the Swiss regions. Jacqueline and Marie looked at the finery they were dressed in, which was much richer than that of their poor dolls from Dörfli or Maienfeld. Uncle Henry once again guessed the wishes of the children. In a nearby shop, he bought for each of the two girls a beautiful doll, all wrapped up in a ribbon, for Elizabeth a necklace made of carved and coloured wooden beads, for Jean-Pierre a horn trumpet, similar to that of Thomas the goatherd, for Robert a long whistle with a shrill sound. In order not to make anyone jealous, he gave his son Jean a tie pin made of Alpine stone and gave his dear mother Heidi a silver filigree brooch.

"What about the little baby Bouby? We have to bring something back to Bouby," said little Marie shyly as she tried to jump on her uncle's neck.

"Good little heart," Heidi remarked; "you're right; we were going to forget our little mountain dwarf."

Uncle Henry bought Bouby a beautiful wooden puppet, articulated.

"And now, the hour passes! I would like to show you some more beautiful flowers and fruit."

"You know, Dad, I don't think the cousins will be very interested in seeing this long gallery; it's quite boring," Jean remarked.

"Come with me," said the uncle, who had his own idea. Indeed, the children and their grandmother passed, indifferent, in front of pyramids of vegetables, displays of various fruits, samples of seeds or straw. They decidedly did not understand why their guide was showing them around this long, endless hall. But they didn't dare to say anything. They walked as fast as they could. It was very hot in this stifling atmosphere. Suddenly they found themselves in the open air, near a landing stage at the foot of the great pylon.

"I've played a good joke on you all," said the uncle laughing. "I admire your discipline. Like good soldiers, you have just made this journey without complaint. Here is the reward: we pass again on the other bank and we will take another ride on the Enchanted River or in the little train, whichever you like best!

"On the river..." was a unanimous cry.

"Good. One more surprise: who wants to come with me up there in the cable car?"

All raised their hands and shouted "me! me! me!." Only little Marie said nothing.

"Don't you want to come with us?"

"Oh no! I would be too scared. I'd rather stay here. I'll wait for you."

"I," says the grandmother, "don't like this kind of transport very much. It seems to me that I'll get dizzy. I'll stay here, waiting for you with Marie."

"I have another solution, Mom. Take the boat with Marie; it approaches at the foot of the other pylon. See you later!"

Words could not describe the feelings of ecstasy felt by the passengers in the nacelle of the cable car. The uncle had to promise them that return would be by the same means.

The second walk on the Enchanted River was even more magnificent than the first... And then minds had to be made up to return to the other bank, so as not to miss the meeting point.

After leaving the "Landi", they left Zurich. The parents, Marie and Robert returned to Maienfeld by train. Uncle Henry took Jean, Elizabeth, Jean-Pierre and Jacqueline by car, as he had promised them. A real party for Annette's two children. For the first few kilometres along Lake Zurich, they were exhilarated by the speed; without saying a word, they saw trees, poles and houses fleeing behind them on the powdery road.

Soon the sun disappeared behind the high hill. Tired, the four children fell asleep. It was already dark when the car stopped in front of Claude's house in Maienfeld...

## CHAPTER TWELVE

## COUNTRY DAY

Today is Swiss Fatherland Day, the 1st of August. The federal flag, a white cross on a red background, is flown at the main mast of Snow White.

In the previous days, under the expert guidance of Grandma Heidi, the children made beautiful, colourful paper garlands. They are long chains with soft and fragile rings.

In the morning, work begins. The chalet must be dressed in festive attire on that day. The children have taken on this fun work. They enthusiastically stretched out the garlands, first at the windows and then at the doors. The goat stable, the dormer windows in the hayloft and even the "green living room" are decorated with them. Cheerfulness reigns everywhere, on the walls, in the trees and in the hearts.

"Daddy! Here comes Daddy," Marie suddenly shouts, who, with all the speed of her little legs, runs to meet Uncle Claude who is climbing the path.

Indeed, the doctor left Maienfeld early, to climb the Alpe and spend this beautiful day in the midst of his family. On the back of his jacket he proudly wears the festive insignia that is being sold throughout Switzerland on this anniversary to raise money for the Red Cross.

At Marie's cry, all the children rushed to the path and gave the unexpected visitor a noisy welcome.

"What's in that big package you're bringing us?" asks Jean.

"A nice surprise for you, if you have been good!"

"They were very obedient and they worked well; look at their work," says said Grandma Heidi, appearing in the doorway and pointing to the lovely garlands.

"Oh! ho! My little friends! It was you who made all these masterpieces? I congratulate you," says Claude.

"We must also thank Grandma, who helped us a little!" says Jacqueline.

"Show us the surprise, uncle Claude."

"Unpack the package!"

"What is it?"

"Patience, little curious ones! Where's your mother? And Edith, and Ida, and everybody? First I want to say hello to them; then we'll unpack the big package. Wait for me in the "green room"; I'll come back to you soon."

The children, although a little disappointed, obeyed. They didn't wait long; Uncle Claude, their mother and Grandma Heidi joined them.

"Cut the string!" cried the little ones, impatiently.

To tease them, Claude undid the knots one by one, quietly rolled the string into a small torch and put it in his pocket. Finally, he opened the mysterious package. He took out seven beautiful new flags and Venetian lanterns. The little ones shouted for joy. What a beautiful party!

"There is a flag and a lantern for everyone."

He unfurled the first flag and handed it to Jean, asking him :

"What is this one, all red, with its little white cross in the corner?"

"The flag of the canton of Schwyz, says Jean as he flies the beautiful flamboyant cloth."

"Bravo! And you, Jean-Pierre, this one, with white and red keys on a background of the same colour?"

"Unterwald."

"I give it to you. And you, Elizabeth, what does this big animal head on a yellow background represent?"

"The bull of Uri."

"It's yours. This one is less known: white with a blue stripe."

"This is the flag of Zug," Jacqueline proudly said.

"Take it, since you are so wise. This is more difficult," said the uncle, floating a blue and white cloth. Who can tell me which canton's emblem it's from?"

"Zurich," says Jacqueline confidently.

"It is for Marie. But, tell me, Jacqueline, do you still know other colours from our townships?"

"Of course, Dad! I know the flags of the 22 cantons of Switzerland."

"Let's have a look. Vaud?"

"Green and white."

" - Fribourg?"

"White and black."

"What about this one, red and yellow?"

"This is Geneva! Give it to Robert."

"The last one, says the uncle, is for little baby Bouby."

And he gave the little one a Swiss flag.

Their eyes sparkled with happiness. Immediately, a procession was improvised. The whole gang, floating the beautiful banners in the luminous air, set off across the pasture singing a lively march.

Today is Homeland Day!

In the afternoon, according to tradition, a bonfire is prepared for lighting in the evening. Grandfather Peter planted a pole in the middle of the large meadow. And all together, big and small, went into the forest in search of dead wood. As they brought it in, Uncle Paul skilfully arranged the dry branches around the pole. The pile grew quickly and soon reached the height of a man. Grandma decided that was enough. Besides, everyone was tired of having made these numerous transports and everyone was happy to rest until the evening meal.

Lina had distinguished herself; the menu was succulent: for dessert, a large bowl of cream and countless small, fragrant and tasty wild strawberries.

The lively conversations were suddenly interrupted by an unexpected visit:

"Good evening to all! I can see that there is nothing boring about "Snow White" on a first August evening."

It was Uncle Henry, believed to be on a business trip to Stuttgart, who suddenly, out of the blue, entered the dining room.

We made way for him. He had a good appetite; he too had a large plate of cream and strawberries.

The children had left the table and, each with their flag in their hands, walked around the chalet and the bonfire, singing at the top of their voices.

"What are you thinking about, Grandma?" said Henry, addressing Heidi. "You look very thoughtful."

"My children, my dear children, you cannot imagine how happy I am. Just now, as I watched the whole family gathered in our chalet, which had become sumptuous, I couldn't help but think of a very old vision: an evening of the first of August, right here. I was a little girl, alone with Uncle de l'Alpe; my bed was a pile of hay, fresh and fragrant, up there in the hayloft. In this very room, where we are, and which you have so admirably transformed, the grandfather's bed, in a corner; in the middle, a table and a chair; that was all."

*In the hearth of the fireplace, Uncle de l'Alpe had lit a large fire; at the end of a long iron fork he had fixed a large piece of cheese which he turned over the hearth to melt and brown it. He had spread this grilled cheese on a piece of bread and filled a cup with goat's milk. This was our festive supper.*

*Then, both of us, alone, we went to sit down towards the three fir trees, which were still very weak; and grandfather had lit his pipe. We didn't say anything; and that was good. We listened, in silence, to the ringing of the bells that went up from the valley. We watched the fire that the mountain people had lit on the Falknis; we contemplated the stars for a long time. Then we returned to the chalet. We were moved, embraced with a strange feeling. I had climbed up to the hayloft and laid down on the hay. Uncle, thinking I was asleep, climbed the ladder, without making a sound; he sat down very close to me. A pale ray, entering through the skylight, lit up his grey beard.*

I opened my eyes. Uncle de l'Alpe was crying softly. And I heard him whispering, chanting the syllables:

"Oh my God, if men knew, if men wanted to! How happy they could be!"

"On that evening of the first of August, we were both alone in the chalet; I was a very little girl... While today... Ah ! My children ! How happy I am !"

This evocation, pronounced in mid-voice, had troubled everyone's soul. A deep silence reigned in the room.

Outside, near the window, the fountain murmured, crystal clear. Further away, the laughter and games of the children livened up the quietness of the evening. Even further away, the call of the little goatherd who was bringing his herd back down to the village resounded.

"We too are happy; and it is thanks to you, my dear Heidi," said Peter, making himself the interpreter of all.

He got up, put a kiss on Granny's forehead and went out to wait for his goats and take them back to the stable.

"I've got a surprise for the little ones," said Henry. "Earlier, I brought a big box containing rockets, sparklers, 'suns' and 'vesuviums'. However, some preparations have to be made in secret: nail the "suns" on poles, put the rockets in the ground, place the Bengal fires on a plank."

"It won't be easy," says Annette. "These devils of kids are snoopers; they stick their noses everywhere; they always have their eyes where they shouldn't have."

"How would you do it?" says Claude. "What do you think, Grandma?"

"Nothing could be simpler: I will gather the children in the "green room". We will prepare the lanterns, then I will tell them stories until the bells ring. This will give you plenty of time to set up your fireworks."

And so it was done. When the seven little ones had fixed the candles in the beautiful paper lanterns, when each had chosen a long forked stick on which to hang the lanterns, and when each had tried out the effect this would have, they sat in a circle around Heidi.

"Grandma," says Robert, "is going to tell the story of William Tell and the evil bailiff once again."

"I," said Jacqueline, "would prefer that of Arnold of Melchtal who, with a stick, broke the fingers of the bailiff's valet who wanted to seize the oxen harnessed to the plough."

"My children," Heidi began, "the events that preceded the founding of the Swiss Confederation have gradually been transformed, embellished, so that it is not always easy to distinguish history from legend. These traditions are based on certain facts; they are part of our national heritage. For six and a half centuries, they have been told in many ways; they have helped to make our country loved."

"Is it true that only three men founded Switzerland?" asked Jean.

"Yes and no. These three men, whose names you certainly know, were not alone. They each represented one of the three valleys."

"Uri, Schwyz and Unterwald," says Elizabeth.

"I see," says Heidi, ""that my little Swiss boys in America know the history of their country. Who taught you?"

"Our teacher, who often reads us beautiful stories at the Swiss school in New York."

"And dad gave us a big book, with lots of pictures."

"Do you know, Jean, what were the names of the first three Confederates?"

"Werner Stauffacher, Walter Fürst and Arnold de Melchtal."

"And," Jean-Pierre added, "it was on the meadow of the Rütli that they swore the first alliance."

"Grandma, tell us the story of the three Swiss," implored Jacqueline; "you know how to tell stories so well."

"You're welcome," says Heidi; "here:"

*Not far from the shore of the tortuous and wild lake of the Four Cantons, in the middle of a forest of fir trees which goes down to the edge of the waves, at the foot of large rocks is a small clearing.*

*It can only be reached from the lake, by boat, or by a steep path that winds its way through the large mountain walls.*

*On the evening of August 1, 1291, the wind blew gently. The grasses of the meadow undulated harmoniously. All you can hear is the regular lapping of the lake waves and the monotonous buzzing of insects. Soon, the night spreads out over the lake; a warm night, full of stars.*

*Suddenly a stone rolled down the path down the mountain. Suddenly, too, you can hear a branch of dead wood cracking in the forest. At the same time, an oar seems to have hit a rock on the bank nearby.*

*Then a mysterious silence envelops the small sloping meadow. Men approach.*

*Those of Uri, carrying their yellow banner with a bull's head, come down the mountain. Those from Schwyz come up from the lake,* preceded by the red flag with a small white cross. Those from Unterwalden come out of the forest, carrying a white and red banner with a silver key shining on it.

They gather in the clearing. Each group has a leader and ten men. They do not speak. The three chiefs come forward, put their swords in the ground and shake hands, saying: "Hail to God".

The oldest of the three chiefs says: "We are determined to live united, as good brothers, loyal and courageous. We swear to sacrifice our lives to preserve the freedom of our homeland and to pass it on intact to our descendants. We pledge to respond to the signal of danger to deliver our valleys from the tyrants who oppress them. The signal, according to the ancient custom of our ancestors, will be fires lit on the peaks of our mountains and on the shores of our lake. May our oath last forever, with God's help! Amen."

Then, in the starry night, the three banners bowed, the thirty-three men uncovered themselves, raised their right hand, two fingers of which were stretched out towards the sky, and said in a single, deep, deaf voice: "I swear!"

The three chiefs shake hands again, promising, on behalf of all, to keep the decisions taken secret. The banners are rolled out slowly. Then, silently, those from Uri climb the mountain path, those from Unterwald go into the thick forest and those from Schwyz get back into their boat and cross the lake.

"Oh!" said Bouby, lifting his little finger. "Granny! Listen!"

During this story, the shadow had spread over the mountains. Dörfli's bell had begun to ring. Further down, the bell of Maienfeld answered it. The sound of other bells, farther away, rose from the bottom of the valley where the lights of the villages and chalets on the slopes of the Alps shone. Soft harmony... One by one, according to the rite, the children's lanterns were lit by Grandma Heidi and one by one, the children went to the pyre where the whole family was gathered.

Suddenly, across the Rhine, a light shone. A fire gave the agreed signal.

"It's Sargans"," says the grandfather. "We can light ours."

On the sloping meadow like the Rütli clearing, the children sat down; their lanterns swayed in the night and lit up their gravely, cheerful faces.

Uncle Paul sets a few dry twigs on fire. In an instant the huge pile of wood ignites and the festive blaze crackles.

One after the other, bonfires are lit everywhere in the region; in Dörfli, in Maienfeld, at the foot of the Grey Horns, at the top of the Piz Sol; and all the way up, on the top of the Falknis, the mountain top, which merges with the stars.

All together, the moving hymns of the country were sung.

The great bonfire of "Snow White" sparkles, throwing orange and blue flames towards the sky. Suddenly, it cracks and bends. Suddenly, it collapses, throwing sparks on all sides that die in the grass.

"In America, asks little Marie, do you also make bonfires?"

"Oh no," answers Elizabeth. "We celebrate the First of August by lighting red, green and white Bengal flames and sending off a few rockets."

"It's a shame we don't have them here," says Jean. "You'd see how beautiful it is."

At that very moment a high-pitched whistle startled everyone and a long streak of light followed by a burst of sound tore through the night.

"A rocket! A rocket!"

The children jumped up and rushed to the place where the light had come from.

They were not even a little bit surprised to find Uncle Henry and Uncle Paul there, amidst poles and thin sticks of white wood planted in the grass.

"Don't come any closer," said Uncle Henry. "Go back and sit next to your parents. I have prepared a wonderful show for you."

A delight of rare splendour awaited the children. Rockets exploded by launching green and then red stars; others projected three sparks in a row, shining like molten silver. The "suns" rotated at breakneck speed, following the red and green blaze of the Bengal flames. Both young and old, sitting in the grass, were shouting with enthusiastic admiration.

Grandma Heidi, sitting by the dying bonfire, hugged Marie and little baby Bouby and whispered: "My God, protect my country. Protect my little ones. Ah! If men knew, if men wanted, how happy humanity would be…"

The last rocket had been fired. The night had advanced. It was time to go to sleep. The children dreamed of stars falling to earth.

## CHAPTER THIRTEEN

## A STORM SUDDENLY BREAKS OUT...

August was coming to an end. The storms that had been raging for several days in a row had forced the children to stay locked in the cottage. The time seemed long to them, although Grandma Heidi did her utmost to invent new games or to tell new stories.

On two Sundays in a row Claude had already been unable to ride from Maienfeld. Henry still had several things to do before he returned to New York with his family.

A wave of sadness lurked on the Alps. In the evening, when the children were in bed, the parents, gathered in the dining room, had nothing to talk about. Or the grandfather, while he was packing the half-smoked tobacco into his pipe, would nod and say:

"Not everything you learn in the newspaper is reassuring. This Danzig affair tells me nothing good."

Then Heidi opened the old Bible and read a comforting passage with fervour. Then she stopped, silent, with her hands joined together.

"Do you remember, Peter, when I came back from Frankfurt and went down from the Alps to the blind grandmother in Dörfli and read beautiful hymns for her?"

"Yes, I remember. You were her ray of joy. And you remained it for us too."

"That would be too awful!" Heidi continued, pursuing her idea. "If the war started again, what would become of the poor mankind? No! The good Lord won't allow that."

That night, dreadful thunderclaps sounded on the Alpe. The children woke up with a start and were seized with terror. A dreadful storm broke out. The rapid lightning flashes were gigantic and the rain whipped the windows of the chalet, which vibrated to the tremendous din of the lightning, whose echoes from the mountain echoed the detonations by prolonging their bearings.

The dawn finally appeared, at first pale. The still dark sky was crossed by heavy clouds; the high rocks looked sinister and threatening. Little by little calm returned. The sun shone warmly on the wet ground. A light steam rose from the pasture and suddenly the Alps were shrouded in a fog so dense that the three fir trees in the "green living room" could hardly be seen from the chalet.

In the meadow the first colchicum had appeared.

It had been decided that the whole family would leave Snow White on the last day of August and go back down to Dörfli at the Manoir House for the night, as Henry and his family were due to leave for New York on 1 September; Claude, Annette and their children would return to Maienfeld.

For two or three days there was a lot of activity in "Snow White" and the departure was prepared.

Regretfully, the gear was collected and the trunks were closed. Grandma Heidi and the children took another nice walk to the rocks where the goats were grazing. Purple gentians with dark foliage and firm flowers exuded their subtle scent. The girls made a magnificent bouquet of them to decorate the "Manoir".

On a clear morning, the whole family walked down the stony path to Dörfli. All together, the children, led by Heidi, walked around the village to greet their friends, whom they hadn't seen all summer. Dinner was eatene early, because it was important to go to bed early that evening. It had been decided that the whole family would go to Maienfeld the next morning to accompany Edith and her children to the station, where they would take the train at eight o'clock; Henry was waiting for them at Uncle Claude's house.

The children had gone up to their rooms and they could be heard chatting with animation.

In the dining room, Pierre had turned the knob on the radio, which hadn't been heard for a long time. The radio was emitting soft music, but the unpleasant sizzling sound was annoying.

"A new storm is brewing somewhere tonight," says Heidi. "This kind of interference in the radio never fools you."

When the piece was finished, the speaker announced: "This is the Swiss national transmitter of Berom Ünster. The Swiss telegraph agency in Bern gives you its newsletter."

"News from Switzerland: The Federal Council, considering that the general political situation has worsened, has just decreed the establishment of border cover troops. Officers, non-commissioned officers, soldiers and complementary services belonging to the units of these troops must enter service immediately. They will go to their places of mobilisation with two days of provisions."

"Finally, that's it!" cried Paul. "I like this better! At least we know what to expect!"

And turning to his wife, he calmly added:

"Ida, prepare the agreed provisions; I will put on my uniform and pack my bag."

He left the dining room, leaving the grandfather and the women petrified. The radio announcer continued to transmit the orders: "The whole Swiss army is on picket duty…." No one in the Manoir House was listening any more. After the first moment of amazement, Annette understood the seriousness of the situation.

"Do you think, grandfather, that this is war?"

"I fear and even dread it."

"What are you so alarmed about," Edith asked, her throat dry.

"You see, my dear children, I have great confidence in our higher authorities. They are wise and far-sighted. Last year, at about the same time as today, mobilization orders had been given in all the countries around us; only Switzerland had not raised any troops, and war did not break out. On the other hand, at the present time, no country has mobilised, as far as I know, and Switzerland is locking its borders. This is significant."

Heidi said, wiping a tear from her trembling cheek. "We don't want to hurt anyone! Why should we?"

"It is not certain that we are affected. Our army is strong, our people are united, our mountains are high and strong, and we are charitable to others," replied the grandfather.

"The Swiss miracle of 1914 to 1918 can be repeated. You have to believe in it," said Ida, standing up. "I'm going to the kitchen to prepare provisions for Paul."

"Claude, who is a first lieutenant doctor, has to leave as well. I am leaving you and going to the post office to phone him," says Annette, nervous.

"And my husband! He was in Zurich until eight o'clock!" added Edith, anxious. "At this very moment he is driving on the road to spend the night at Claude's house in Maienfeld; what will become of him? Surely he hasn't heard the news yet! I will call Annette on the phone. Will we even be able to go back to New York? Our places are booked on the liner leaving Le Havre the day after tomorrow."

"Henry is still old enough to serve," the grandfather remarked. "The army is setting up a picket line. No Swiss citizen is, until further notice, allowed to leave his country."

"But, it's awful!" cried Edith, rushing outside.

Heidi, left alone with Peter, took the old Bible, opened it quietly at the page marked with a pink bookmark and read it:

"You who love the Lord abhor evil: He protects the lives of His faithful and delivers them from the hand of the wicked."

She added, with her hands clasped together and her eyes closed: "My God, take this bitter cup away from the lips of your poor children! My God, protect my country!"

At that moment, a drum roll suddenly sounded under the windows and the town crier read the order to mobilise the frontier cover troops.

In an instant the whole of Dörfli was in turmoil. You could hear fast footsteps pounding the cobblestones of the small square. Calls:

"Georges, we have to go and tell dad and uncle right away,"

"Wait, Mrs Schneider, Louis will go up with his friend Georges. They will make the detour through the forest, to announce the news to my husband and his cousin, who are on the mountain pasture."

All this unusual noise had awakened the children of the "Manoir". In slippers, they had rushed first to the windows, then into the corridor where they had met Paul, in uniform, bag on his back, rifle on his shoulder, who was going down to the kitchen.

"Daddy! Daddy! Daddy! Where are you going, shouted little Robert. You didn't say you had to go to military service!"

Little Marie, instinctively, cried. Jean admired the beautiful golden buttons on the tunic.

A few minutes later everyone was gathered in the kitchen where Lina was busy wrapping bread, cheese, bacon, dried meat, fruit and a few lumps of sugar in paper. Ida packed as much fresh butter as she could into an aluminium tin, rinsed the enamel gourd and filled it with red wine.

In the meantime Annette and Edith had returned from the post office, feeling sorry: it was impossible to reach Maienfeld by telephone; the lines were already militarised.

"But I can't let Claude go away like that, all alone, without having kissed him," said Annette. "And then, he must need me. A man alone doesn't know how to manage household affairs. I have to help him pack his officer's bag."

"A soldier's bag is quicker to buckle," says Ida, repressing a bitter smile.

"As for me," says Edith, "I also have to go down to Maienfeld to find out what's happening with Henry.

"But I, too, have to go down to Maienfeld; that's my gathering place," says Paul, who calmly, methodically, as if at an inspection, checked whether his bag contained all the prescribed items.

"The simplest thing is for all four of us to go down together," concludes the grandfather, who, in his heart of hearts, was not unhappy to find this pretext to go to the city in search of more precise news. "I'm going to harness the cart, it's better; because at night, the vineyard path would not be very convenient for Edith; she's not used to the mountains."

Lina, with foresight, prepared a large pot of boiling black coffee. We sat down again around the common table. The children, sensing that the moment was solemn, were silent.

"What consoles me," says Annette, "is that our two soldiers are not going far. They are staying close to us, in the border region. We may have the opportunity to see them often."

"And then," Paul added, putting down his empty cup, "it won't last long. Maybe it's just an alert."

"The cart is ready; we have to leave," said the grandfather as he returned to the room.

The children, moved, embraced the soldier who left them so suddenly to go and defend them. They accompanied him to the garden gate. A moment later, the cart plunged into the night.

# CHAPTER FOURTEEN

## A CHARITABLE IDEA

Winter, in the mountains, is not a sad season. On the shiny, glittering snow, the sun shines above the thick fog that covers the valley bottoms. The firs jealously guard their greenery; the fine larches profile their golden needles and some trees remain adorned with their autumn red foliage.

Some evenings, the humid atmosphere takes on fantastic hues at dusk, with gold, mauve and blue, while the summits are coloured orange or fiery red.

All the fathers were under arms. Uncle Henry himself, surprised by the general mobilisation while he was in Switzerland, had had to announce himself and he had been drafted into the engineering corps. After some time he could have been dismissed and returned to America, but he did not want to leave his family, whose transport would have been dangerous. He preferred to stay in Switzerland, mobilised. Edith and her two children had settled in the "Manoir House". Annette went back down to Maienfeld with Jean-Pierre and

Jacqueline, but they went back up to Dörfli as often as possible on Sundays and during school holidays.

From the first day of September, troops had occupied the village, which is very close to the border. The captain and his officers were staying with the vicar; the soldiers' quarters had been established in all available premises. The military kitchen was set up in the laundry room of the "Manoir House".

For the children, it was a joy to do small favours for the soldiers. They were not a little proud when the cook allowed them to taste the troop's soup or chocolate.

The grandfather had joined the troops of the Passive Air Defence; he was often on guard, so that the whole weight of the household rested on Granny Heidi.

At night she would gather the children together in the dining room and supervise their school work; her experience was a great help to the little schoolchildren who made rapid progress under her guidance.

Often, once the homework was done, she would tell one of those beautiful stories she had the secrets to.

The days grew longer and longer, the snow melted and spring returned.

This "phony war" seemed to last for centuries. When, suddenly, on a clear May morning, the radio announced the invasion of Holland and then of Belgium, anguish blew like a storm over the small Swiss homeland. The General recalled all the soldiers from the army. The country was in danger, the borders threatened.

Anxiously we listened to the newsletters. France was invaded... mainland France laid down its arms.

"Grandma," asked Robert, one evening when the atmosphere was particularly overheated, "do you think they'll come to our house too?"

"Our soldiers will know how to stop them," says Elizabeth confidently.

"Daddy is a good shot; he has a machine gun," added little Marie.

"Say, Grandma," continued Jean, "have you seen the little cannon that is pointed over the road, on the path of 'Snow White'? The corporal told me that each shot would destroy a tank."

"Our soldiers will do as in Morgarten: they will throw rocks and tree trunks at them when they are close by."

"My little ones, let's have confidence," replied Granny Heidi. "The good Lord, who has often saved us from great misfortunes, will watch over us this time too. Switzerland is a charitable country. It will heal wounds and relieve misery, if war does not reach it. Go to bed and sleep in peace!"

***

The month of June was splendid. The flowers looked more beautiful than in previous years, the meadows seemed greener.

Every morning the goatherd led his herd to the pasture. At the "Manoir" the children were gloomy.

"We don't know if we will be able to go up to the Alpe chalet this summer, the grandfather had said. "Snow White" serves as a cantonment for a half-section and the captain is unwilling to withdraw the soldiers because," he said, "its situation is wonderful for an observation post and for a machine gun position."

"Never mind," says Jean resignedly, "it's not that far off. We'll go up in the morning and come down in the evening."

"Good idea!" said Elizabeth. "We'll go up with the goats and come down with them. Granny will prepare the picnic."

"Will Aunt Annette, Jean-Pierre and Jacqueline come to Dörfli?" asked Marie.

"I hope so," replied Granny. "Uncle Claude will soon have a fortnight's leave which he plans to spend here with his family."

"Then we'll all be together again, just like last summer," says Robert.

"Except Daddy!" exclaimed Jean, Elizabeth and Marie together.

"It's true," observed Granny.

A few days later, two pieces of happy news arrived at the same time: the soldiers would evacuate "Snow White" on the following Saturday for the whole summer, and Uncle Claude and his family would go up to Dörfli on the following Sunday.

On that day, everyone moved to the chalet on the Alpe, as they had done the previous year.

The greatest joy of the children was to go on an excursion with Claude, because on the way he would talk to them about what he had seen in military service. And Uncle Claude was an officer! Never had his prestige been so great.

One morning when they had climbed up to the "goat rocks" together and sat down on the thick grass, Claude told them:

"You can't imagine how happy you are, my little ones. If you only knew how many children your age suffer in invaded countries. A

Swiss colonel, sent to France on a mission by the Red Cross, gave us medical officers a lecture last week. He had gone to Lille."

"It's in the north of France, very close to Belgium," says Jean-Pierre.

"You are right, my son, you are strong in geography. Well, around Lille, the colonel saw hundreds of little children whose houses had been destroyed or looted. Most of them no longer know where their mothers are."

"What about their dads?" asked Jacqueline.

"But they are at war," says Jean.

"Not quite," Claude corrected. "They are prisoners and have been taken to camps."

"It's very sad not to have a mum or dad any more," says Marie.

"Fortunately they have their grandmother and grandfather," remarked Robert, who could not conceive of a small child being alone on earth.

"Alas! Very often they no longer have them; neither uncle nor aunt!" said Claude.

"So how do they sleep and eat?" Elizabeth asked.

"We don't always know," replied the uncle. "That's why the Red Cross is sending doctors and nurses to help these unfortunate little ones. They are given food parcels and medicines, because many of them are sick. Often even a few are killed or wounded by the bombing."

The children were silent, pensive. The goats in the surrounding area rang their bells as if to call their little friends who so often played with them. That day, neither Jean, Elizabeth, Marie nor the others wanted to have fun. They were thinking of the little children who are all alone in a big, devastated city, of little children their age who are hungry and killed by the bombs.

Claude thought to himself: "I am only a blundering fool; I saddened these little new hearts when they are just begging to beat, joyful, in the middle of such a beautiful landscape, on such a radiant day." He wondered by what means he could divert their imagination from these lamentable visions, when Jean-Pierre broke the silence:

"They should come to Switzerland. Houses are not destroyed there! There is no war; there are no bombs. We would share meals with them."

"Good little heart!" says Claude. "You're not alone in thinking that way. The Committee of the Red Cross, with the work called "Swiss Children's Relief", has just taken steps to send us the most unfortunate ones."

"Will they come to Dörfli?" asked Jacqueline eagerly.

"I don't know. It depends," replied her father.

"It depends on what?"

"The Red Cross will launch an appeal as soon as it knows whether its proposal has been accepted. It will ask if any Swiss families want to take in these small refugees."

"Could we get one at "Snow White"?" Marie asked.

"You are already seven children here; that's a lot," says Claude.

"One more, it won't be known, as we will share," said Jean. "We'll ask Granny; she'll say yes, I'm sure!"

"It's likely," says Claude, "Let's go back down to the chalet and ask him together."

The little troop took a good step down the path, under the disappointed eyes of the young goats, who couldn't understand why, that day, their little friends had abandoned them.

# CHAPTER FIFTEEN

## DIDIER, A CHILD FROM ALSACE

Maienfeld railway station is very lively. On the square there are about ten country floats parked. The horses, harassed by the flies, shake their long tails and shake their heads in a bad mood, making the bells of their collars chime. It looks like a market day.

On the arrival platform, farmers, mountain people and children are chatting briskly.

The waiting room is closed. Through the glass door you can see, inside, a doctor's officer - it's Claude - a nurse and four scouts.

Suddenly, the automatic bell rings its double tinkling three times: ding, dong; ding, dong; ding, dong! The Sargans train is announced. The stationmaster with the red cap comes out of his office, the green and white palette in his hand.

"Back, please. Attention!"

A few minutes later, the train arrives in a hurry, the brakes squeak; the convoy slows down and stops with remarkable precision. From a beautiful half-empty carriage, marked with the sign "Reserved", a nurse and a dozen pale and flabbergasted-looking children get off the train. Some of them carry a musette with a shoulder strap, others hold a suitcase or a large package in their hands.

A large cardboard label with letters, a number and other inscriptions hangs around the neck of each one. They are little French children from Alsace, part of a convoy of three hundred refugees who had arrived in Basel the night before.

First Lieutenant Claude greets the nurse who leads them, shakes her hand cordially and leads the whole group to the waiting room.

"I'd like to know who ours is," says Jean.

"In any case, it's a boy; Uncle Claude has promised to give us a boy and not a girl," added Elizabeth.

"Did you notice the little blond boy, curly, with the Basque beret? He looks very nice, says Jacqueline. Daddy will choose him for us, no doubt."

The families who had registered to receive one of these unfortunate young people in their home waited patiently for the first formalities to be completed.

It didn't take long. The officer, with a list in his hand, reappeared on the station platform.

"One person per family will enter the room. The others will wait for their little protégé in the square, just outside the station."

Then he made the call. Annette entered the station room. In the square, there was a crowd. All the inhabitants of Maienfeld, even those who were not expecting anyone, had come to show their sympathy to the children of France. Several had brought a basket of beautiful, firm and appetizing cherries, picked that very morning; others held a few chocolate bars in their hands to give to the little refugees.

It was almost four o'clock in the afternoon; the sun was still very hot. Between the stretchers of their carriage, the horses, impatient, were hammering with their shoddy hooves the sound and burning pavement.

Finally the door opened and the "godparents" and "godmothers" came out one after the other, holding their child by the hand. Each one joined his or her adoptive family, while the inhabitants of the village cheerfully distributed the sweets.

Annette went out last, with her husband, framing the little blond, curly boy that Jacqueline had noticed.

"This is your new companion," Claude tells the assembled children. "His name is Didier and he speaks a little German. I'm sure you'll make a good match."

"My name is Jacqueline;" and she kissed him gently.

"And me, Jean."

"And me, Marie."

Everyone named themselves and shook Didier's hand with cordiality. Didier, dumbfounded by such a friendly welcome, stretched out his weary little hand. His blue eyes shone with a bright glow of love and gratitude. He was silent.

"We will go home first," says Claude, "where a good snack awaits us. Grandpa will drive the car there. As for us, we will go on foot. It's five minutes away; it'll make your legs a bit tired, my little guy!"

"Thank you, officer," said Didier finally.

He had a clear, timbrous, slightly dragging and singing voice that immediately won over his new friends.

Jean grabbed Didier's big bag. Jacqueline and Elizabeth took the little French boy by the hand and in the blink of an eye the children formed a large group which ran the entire width of the road.

The whole family, including the nurses and scouts that mamy had invited, rushed to the doctor's villa.

"Mademoiselle," Didier slipped in the ear of the nurse who had accompanied him during the trip and who, as a result, was no longer a complete stranger to him,

"Mademoiselle, I would like to wash my hands and face before going to the table."

"Nothing is easier and more natural, my child."

She led to Didier's bathroom who kept repeating: "How beautiful it is here! How beautiful!"

Everyone was at the table when the little refugee returned. The children applauded in a welcoming manner.

"Sit there," says Annette. "You must be hungry."

"Oh yes, thank you very much, Madam."

"Don't say "Madame", but Aunt Annette, or Mamy, as your little friends call me. You would like that, wouldn't you?"

"Yes, Mrs. Mamy!"

The children laughed out loud at this unexpected and comical response.

Didier, confused, felt like crying. He looked at the table set up and couldn't believe his eyes: two jars full of milk and coffee; a sugar bowl full of sugar; countless slices of bread, butter, honey...

"Come on, big boy! Be as cheerful as this band of mischievous people. You'll see how much we'll like you," said Granny Heidi, who occupied the place of honour at the end of the imposing table.

"I can already feel it," Didier whispered with a smile.

"Drink your cup of café au lait, eat this toast with butter and honey. It's Dörfli honey; taste how sweet it is," said Jacqueline, who had been placed next to the child.

Didier, embarrassed to feel the focus of all these strangers, bit with his lips. Claude, who was watching him, said to him:

"My fellow, follow the example of the children around you who are already on their second buttering! From now on, you are a relative, brother or cousin of these kids, as you please, and when you are upstairs, from tonight on, consider yourself at home. Is that understood?"

"Yes, Officer."

Didier, turning to Jacqueline, asked shyly :

"So I won't be staying in this beautiful villa? Where is it, 'up there'?"

Jacqueline pointed out the high rocks of Falknis from the window.

"'Up there' is the mountain, in the "Snow White" chalet above Dörfli."

Didier turns pale. He suddenly remembered a story that his teacher had read in class just before the war, about Swiss shepherds climbing up steep rocks, crossing dangerous walls and bending over dizzying abysses. One of them had slipped in search of the beautiful flowers of the Alps and two days later his mutilated body was found at the bottom of a torrent.

"Why do we have to go "up there"?" he says in a white voice. "I don't want to go to the precipice; I'm afraid!"

"Don't be afraid," says Grandma Heidi in a gentle and reassuring tone. "The chalet where we live is surrounded by beautiful meadows and peaceful forests. The precipices are much further away; we never go there."

"I think it's time to leave," said the grandfather. "Say goodbye to Uncle Claude, who is due to rejoin his battalion again this evening. Thank him for his generous snack. I will hitch up the car and wait for you at the gate."

It was now cooler; a light breeze passed over the mountainside. The carriage was well loaded; the horse was slowly riding up the road with its many bends. The conversation started between Didier and Heidi's grandchildren; little by little, the young Frenchman felt more at ease and no longer answered only with monosyllables! The lively air whipped his face and already his cheeks had turned pink.

"How old are you?"

"Ten years."

"Like me," says Jean-Pierre. "Do you also have a sister?"

"Yes; she is thirteen years old; her name is Marguerite."

"Did she also come to Switzerland?"

"Oh no! She stayed with Mum."

"You still have your mummy," Elizabeth said, astonished, because she had though that all the little French refugees no longer had a mother.

"Of course; she works at the munitions factory."

"What about your dad?"

Didier sighed loudly.

"Daddy! We don't know where he is anymore; we haven't heard from him for three months."

"Maybe he's a prisoner!" says Marie.

"We don't know... I don't know..."

"You tire Didier with all your questions," said Grandma Heidi. "Talk about something else, about what he sees here for the first time, for example."

"You see that river shining down there like silver," explained Jean-Pierre the geographer, "it's the Rhine."

"The Rhine!" exclaimed Didier in amazement. "Near us, there is also a river called the Rhine. But it is not the same!"

"Yes, it's the same. It flows through Switzerland, forms its northern boundary and leaves our country in Basel."

"In Basel!" Didier said, more and more surprised; "In Basel where we were this morning?"

"Yes, from Basel, the Rhine flows towards your country, Alsace."

This revelation comforted the heart of the little Frenchman. He rejoiced at the thought that this same water, which he saw passing through the river at the moment, his mother and sister would no doubt see it in their turn in a few hours! The Rhine would henceforth be for him a link that would connect him to the loved ones he had abandoned.

Jean gave the names of the villages and peaks that could be seen in the surrounding area; Jacqueline and Elizabeth pointed out the bright flowers whose names Uncle Paul had taught them all. This made the road to Dörfli seem short. We got out of the car and entered the "Manoir House" for a few moments.

"Do you feel the strength to walk three quarters of an hour to the chalet, my little man?" asked Grandma to Didier.

"Oh yes, Grandma, I'm not tired."

"You will see the pretty path we are going to follow; and then, rest assured: there are no precipices!"

"With all of you, I am not afraid. You are so good to me."

Mamy gave each one a roll, a bar of chocolate and a good cup of raw, creamy and fragrant milk, which had just been milked. Then we set off.

Didier never stopped admiring all the flowers smiling at him on the edge of the path.

"Oh! The pretty little blue flower! with its all-white heart. It looks like a star!"

"That's a gentian," says Jacqueline.

"Can I take it? Is it allowed?"

"All the flowers you like are yours; here, I give it to you," answered Elizabeth, picking the gentian and handing it to Didier. "Tomorrow, we will go and make a beautiful bouquet together."

Towards the middle of the journey, Didier stopped, listening:

"Do you hear all those bells in the mountains? It sounds like the chime of a belfry."

"These are the goats coming down from the Alps."

Soon, the cheerful little goats appeared, jumping and bouncing all over the place. The graceful beasts greeted their little friends in their own way, bleating and licking their hands. Some of them, curious and intrigued, approached Didier who was unknown to them. In the blink of an eye the herd surrounded the little Frenchman who, frightened, raised his arms as high as he could, trying to get away. The most daring stood up on their hind legs and put their front hooves on the shoulder of the child, which almost knocked him over.

Thomas, the goatherd, cracked his whip vigorously and brought order to his unruly horde, which he led towards the village.

We went up again and soon we were within sight of the chalet; at the turn of the path, it appeared, lit by the last rays of the sun.

"Here we are," said Grandma. "I congratulate you, my little man. You walked like a mountain man."

Didier stopped abruptly, tore off his Basque beret from his head and froze motionless, all pale and trembling in the middle of the path.

The children, stunned, looked at him, anxious. Grandma Heidi and Annette, worried, wondered what was happening so suddenly to their protégé.

"What's the matter, darling? But what's the matter with you?" Heidi repeated, tapping on the suddenly sweaty cheeks. "Do you feel ill? Answer me."

Didier, prey to a violent emotion, reached out his arm in the direction of the chalet and said with a sob:

"There! Can't you see it? Right there!"

"Calm down, my child. This is "Snow White", this is our chalet..."

"No! Not that! There, at the mast, can't you see it? A blue, white, red flag: a French flag. Oh mummy, oh my daddy…"

Didier threw himself into Granny's arms and sobbed without holding back any longer.

It was Lina who had the touching idea to hoist a French flag on the main mast below the Swiss flag, on the same rope! The shock had been too violent for the brave child who had unexpectedly found himself in the presence of his country's colours. There, at home, he was forbidden to fly them, on pain of death. Mamy had taken Didier in her arms and carried him to the chalet.

"Quickly, Lina, a cup of hot, very sweet coffee. It will comfort him."

Didier quickly recovered from his big outburst of emotion. Grandma took him to the room he would share with Jean and Jean-Pierre. A wooden bed, decorated with pretty polychrome patterns was reserved for him. Beautiful white sheets, a puffy quilt covered with a red and white checkered filling; on the pillow, folded, a nightdress with embroidered blue festoons.

The long, memorable day, full of incidents, had been tiring for everyone.

The evening meal was calm; everyone was tired. Lina had prepared her favourite dessert: delicious cream and tasty wild strawberries which everyone, and Didier in particular, enjoyed. That evening, the children didn't hesitate to go to bed.

As usual, the grandfather, after lighting his pipe, inspected the cottage, carefully closed the doors and returned to sit in his armchair in the dining room where Heidi, Mamy, Edith and Ida were waiting for him, conversing in low voices.

***

On the Alpe, at the beginning of summer, the day lasts a long time, the soft light lingers. At "Snow White", the lamps had not yet been turned on. In the half-light, Heidi and the three mothers exchanged their thoughts, with open arms.

"Of course, he's all out of place, our little protégé."

"He seems very nice."

"Well-mannered, in any case."

"Three months passed quickly."

"Claude has chosen a good companion for our children."

"I noticed it immediately among her classmates this morning," says Annette.

"Jacqueline too; while waiting in the square, she was already talking about the little blond boy, curly, with the Basque beret and blue eyes," Heidi added.

"We won't be able to let the tricolour flag fly all summer at the main mast; I'll take it down early tomorrow morning," remarked the grandfather. "A decree of the Federal Council forbids the display of foreign colours."

"It will hurt him," says Edith.

"I have an idea, suggested Heidi. I'll put this flag in his room, against the wall, above his bed."

"He has to be happy here!"

"And it will be…"

At that moment, the bedroom door opened very gently and Jean-Pierre, barefoot, in his nightgown, appeared on the threshold.

"Mamy, Mamy, the little French boy must be very sad. I heard him crying, his head buried under his pillow. I don't know what to say to console him. He didn't realise that I came down to you. Come and see…"

"I'll ride with you," said Grandma.

They both entered the bedroom without making a sound, from which loud sobs were heard. Jean-Pierre slipped under his sheet and Heidi stood, for a silent moment, at the foot of Didier's bed. Then, slowly approaching, she raised the pillow, saying mischievously:

"Peekaboo, Didier, peekaboo!"

The child smiles through his tears. Granny added, most naturally:

"Come on, darling, you don't sleep with your head under the pillow, you could choke!"

And pretending to be surprised, she added:

"How! How did this happen! You cried! Did Jean-Pierre or Jean quarrel with you? Did they upset you?"

"Oh, no! Ma'am. They fell asleep right away."

"Are you unhappy with us? Tell me, what's wrong?"

"Nothing, ma'am."

"Do not say "Madam". You know you have to call me Grandma; you will be my grandson during your stay in Switzerland."

The child did not respond. Large tears began to run down his hollow cheeks again.

"At least you're not sick," said Heidi, "putting the back of her hand on the boy's forehead. Are you missing something? Answer me."

The child looked up with his big, bright, moist eyes and looked into Granny's good eyes. He hesitated. At last, in a murmur, he said:

"Mummy, my mummy!"

"Brave little heart! You are thinking of your mother, as she is certainly thinking of you at the moment. Don't you think she would be happy to know that her dear Didier is well looked after, safe from danger and misery."

"Oh yes!"

"Do you want me to try to replace her here?"

Didier took Heidi's hands and drew her towards him. The grandmother understood what the child wanted.

"Your mummy sits on the edge of your bed every night, just like that, doesn't she? And then, with your hands joined together, like this, you say in one voice: "My God, protect my daddy, make sure he comes back soon. Protect our soldiers and our country". And every night we will add: "Protect my mum and make her happy, amen!"

Didier was no longer crying. His eyes closed; Heidi leaned towards him and said quietly:

"And your mummy, every evening, kisses you tenderly on the forehead, like I do."

Didier stretched out his arms; affectionately he took Granny by the neck, held her tight and gave her a big kiss on the cheek.

"Thank you, Mummy Granny! I like you…"

He fell asleep peacefully. Heidi, moved in spite of herself, remained for many more minutes contemplating her protégé.

"And to think, she sighed, that there are thousands of little Didiers around the world!"

On tiptoe, in the darkness, grandmother Heidi withdrew, radiant with joy.